SPIN
the
BOTTLE
for
LOVE ♡

*"Comfy, beach read, New adult
Romance full of friendship and heart"*

Elle Oaks

First Edition: June 2023

ISBNs:

979-8-9871958-4-0 (paperback)

979-8-9871958-5-7 (ebook)

For more content by this author, go to:

elleoaks.com

Send inquiries to author at

Gmail: elleoaksco@gmail.com

Or contact via form on elleoaks.com

Chapter One

"Just spin the bottle! Do it and I'll leave you alone forever. I promise."

Her last words left in a drunken slur. I rolled my eyes and continued to study my chemistry book. My frizzy brown hair and split, pink tips fell in front of my face, but I refused to move them. I didn't want the group to see my flustered cheeks. My heart rate always accelerated when they acknowledged my existence, as a form of bullying or teasing would often follow.

"Should have escaped when I had the chance..." I said under my breath.

They always locked the doors after they're all in, not wanting the dorm supervisor to get a peek at what was really going on.

Sara stood up from the circle, the others giggled and murmured. As she tried to step over one of her friends, she stumbled as her foot failed to lift past their knee. A beer bottle tipped, fizz bubbling onto the carpet. The group bit their lips in a fit to hold back their laughter. Sara vehemently shushed them.

"Alex, please," Sara knelt at her bedside and interlocked her fingers. "Pleeeeease."

"Fine."

They all knew from my tone that I was frustrated, but this only riled them up more. I pushed my book from my lap and slid my legs off the bed. Shooing Sara from my bedside, I sighed and trudged toward their cult-like circle. I lowered myself to the ground with crossed legs and took a deep breath. My heart raced as the thought of actually having to kiss one of them with their alcohol-laced breath would bring regret not only to myself but to the unfortunate soul should they remember it.

My fingertips touched the cold, glass bottle, sending a chill up my spine. With a swift movement of my hand, the bottle spun.

Round. And round. And round it went.

Sara leaned over my shoulder and fell onto my back as she lost her balance. My head lurched forward with my hair covering the view. All I heard was the resounding "Oooh." I looked up and followed the neck of the stopped bottle to my victim.

"Chase."

Sara blinked a couple of times before waking up to the reality, sense breaking through her fuzzy brain.

"Wowowoah," she said, attempting a serious tone but falling short. "That can't be right."

"Rules are rules, Sara," Miguel said as he leaned to the side to place an arm around Bridgette's shoulder.

"There's no going against the divine bottle," Bridgette agreed, and she flirtatiously eyed Miguel up and down.

"No, no, no. He's not even technically in the circle. No one is to kiss him but me."

"The bottle cares not of relationships," said Brian, a philosophy major who always held an arrogant tone. Everyone knew he was only in the popular group for his rich parents, but he didn't care. "The bottle only cares about the truth."

"Well, your truth can bite my ass!"

"It's fine," I said standing up with my hands in the air. "I didn't want to play anyways."

My eyes moved around the circle and landed on Chase. He stared at the floor in front of him with the semblance of a small grin on his face. It was hard not to look at his muscular calves as he leaned his toned arm on his knee. His bronze skin, tanned by the many hours he spent in the sun at soccer practice, glowed. I blushed, thinking that I almost had to kiss an Apollo look-alike. Even worse was the fact that he's Sara's boyfriend.

"That's not how this works," Miguel stated, popping the tab of another beer. He took a gulp. "You don't have a choice. The bottle has chosen. Even if it's just a little peck."

"No."

"Yes!" Cassidy yelled, making the group jump. "Listen. They'll just wander into the closet, close the door, and do it there. That way you don't have to see, and we won't be cursed for disobeying the bottle."

"You all are crazy," Sara pouted.

She crossed her arms and took a seat with her back facing the group. After a moment of silence, through which I stood paralyzed, Sara released a dramatic sigh.

"Fine. Go. Go!" Her eyes connected with Chase's as she pointed at the closet. "Just get it over with."

Chase rolled his eyes and stood up. My eyes widened, not believing that he would actually go through with this. He grabbed the handle of the closet door and turned to me.

"Are you coming?"

I nodded.

We entered the closet. Luckily both of us were thin, but I felt a hanger piercing the back of my head. He closed the door behind him, pushing his body nearer to mine as the closing door limited our space. His body heat permeated through the thick darkness, his warm breath sweeping the hair from the front of my face. I looked to the ground and picked at my fingers, nerves crawling about my skin.

"You don't have to do this," I whispered, my shaky voice making my nerves all the more evident.

He turned on the flashlight of his cellphone and threw it to the ground. The light worked wonders with the shadows to enhance his muscular form and sharp jawline. His eyes twinkled like stars at the darkest hour. His hand found my lower back and I licked my lips.

"I'm so sorry it landed on you. But you really don't have to."

He lowered his head near mine, as he stood almost six inches taller than me.

"May I?"

"Yes."

Chase placed a hand behind my head and pulled me in for the kiss.

I lost myself. Whether we kissed for an hour or only a second, time no longer existed and all else disappeared. His smooth upper lip slipped into my mouth, my lower lip into his. I tensed as my hormones skyrocketed, hoping he wouldn't notice my temperature rising. My desire to kiss him forever, and my fear of pulling away before he was ready to let go, froze me to place.

My foot fidgeted and kicked his cellphone against the door of the closet. The bang sucked us back to reality and he pulled away. Chase changed his expression from soft to serious in a moment and opened the closet door. After I exited, he bent over to pick up his phone.

"You were in there for like four seconds," Miguel laughed, mocking us.

"Yeah," Cassidy said, grabbing the beer from Miguel's hand. "Did you like even kiss?"

"If you want to believe we did, that's fine," Chase answered calmly.

Sara smirked and eyed me, as if toying with me. I rolled my eyes and grabbed my bag and phone. The group laughed at the thought of us being too embarrassed to kiss one another. Little did they know...

I climbed around the group and walked out, them shouting to hurry and close the door. I heard more fizz fall to the carpet as the door shut behind me, shaking my head about the mess I would have to clean up in the morning.

Hey

I texted Jordyn, my best friend on campus. Praying she would soon respond, I headed toward where I assumed her to be on a Friday night: The Lounge.

The music was loud, the crowd barely existent except for those pumped for the amateur groups. Jordyn was one of those.

She stood with her elbows leaning on the stage, swaying back and forth, her phone vibrating on the table behind her. The painted curtain behind the band read "Spoon Fed," no doubt some kind of angst-y rock group with death metal type lyrics for not being understood. Jordyn loved that type of shit.

I pulled on her sleeve, and she jumped with a snarl.

"You bitch," she whispered, pushing me away from the stage so as to not disrupt the performance for the other three people listening. She grabbed my hand and led me to the bar. It was a juice bar, but with the same aesthetic of any other.

"I'll take a carbo spritzed lemonade with cherry and strawberry flavor." She turned to me. "My treat. What do you want?"

My hand went to my turning stomach, the butterflies performing somersaults and flips within. I shook my head.

"Come on."

Silence.

"Get her a creamy orange with a scoop of vanilla ice cream."

The bartender worked his magic to make our drinks. A student on campus no doubt focusing more on mixology than his actual studies. Probably only at this school to appease his parents or escape them, like I did.

"What's up?" Jordyn asked.

As I went to answer, she twirled around, screamed, and applauded as the song ended. I jokingly rubbed my ear.

"What? That was like my favorite song of the set."

"Oh yeah," I giggled. "What's it called?"

She licked her lips and laughed.

"I don't know but it's probably some masochistic, emo, shit name."

"Yeah, probably."

The sound of glass meeting wood grabbed our attention. Jordyn slid the cash across the counter, winked at the bartender, and led me to her table. We sat and Jordyn checked her phone to see the message I sent previously.

"Oops."

My fingertips tapped the cold glass of my beverage. I couldn't possibly drink it, not with how unsettled I still felt. But not just that, if I closed my eyes, I could still taste him. His lips left this lingering sweet taste from the cherry soda he had been sipping throughout the night. The sensation was a ghost in my memory, causing my entire body to tense at the thought.

Jordyn put her phone on the table and stared at me until I acknowledged her.

"What?"

"Weren't you supposed to be studying for that huge exam you have next week?"

"I was, but-"

"You said, I can't go out tonight, too busy teehee. Remember?"

"Yes..."

"And aren't you normally asleep by this time?"

"Okay now you're just being dramatic."

Jordyn gasped and raised a hand to her chest.

"Me? Never."

After a moment of wearing straight expressions, we both broke. She sucked at the straw of her beverage, all the while eyeing me. I guess it was my turn.

"Something crazy happened tonight."

"Ooh, drama. Let's hear it."

I looked around, as if thinking someone would possibly be eavesdropping. I shook my head.

"So, I somehow got pulled into their drunken antics."

"Whoa whoa whoa. You're talking about Sara and Co. Right?"

"Yeah."

"Ooh. Juicy, juicy."

"They were playing spin the bottle and..."

"Who did you kiss?"

I took a breath and stared into her eyes. She was about to jump from her seat, make a scene.

"Chase."

"What?!?"

Jordyn jumped from her chair and fell to the ground. Glares arrived at them from some of the other patrons. The singer of the band stumbled over a couple of words but managed to pick back up. I just rolled my eyes.

"Oh my. Was it good? How long? How good? How did Sara react? Oh, she must have been so pissed." Jordyn, who was once again in her chair, grabbed the edges of her seat and kicked her legs in excitement.

With the weight finally off my chest, I decided I could no longer wait to take a sip. The orange was so fresh as it hit my tastebuds. This would be the taste I remember from our kiss. This drink would forever hold the memory. A slight smile crept onto my face.

Jordyn licked her lips and propped her head up with her hands under her chin and elbows on the table. She batted her eyelids at me.

"You're in love."

I choked in the second tasting of the drink. I felt the cream hit the back of my nostrils.

"What?"

"You are so in love! I can see it now. You and Chase going on a picnic at the park. Taking pictures at a zoo. He's such a genuine guy. You're totally a better fit for him than that 'cheerleader who peaked in high school' type."

"Okay, no need to take shots at her. After all, I am the one crushing on her boyfriend."

"And that's totally fair. You're totally right. But you did kind of kiss him."

"It was forced."

"So, no consent?"

"Maybe a little..."

"Well, well, well," Jordyn clicks her tongue and puts on an accent. "Looks like we've got a conundrum here, boys."

I laughed but deep inside I knew she was right. Even if feelings were reciprocated, he was still with Sara. As long as the two remained together, there was no way I'd be in that equation. And no way I was going to act like joining the next game of spin the bottle just for another chance.

It was no more than fantasy. No more than my hormones taking over. I would have to let it be no more than a distant memory. A memory I could enjoy. But it would never go any further.

"Alright, we're done talking about it. Let's just enjoy the music."

"Damn right we will! You're gonna forget all about that soccer star babe when you see the lead singer of the next band. Mmm, he's a treat!"

Jordyn leaps from her seat and takes to the stage. I stay back and sip at my drink, trying to enjoy every bit as I say goodbye to the memory I know will try to return to haunt me.

Chapter Two

During class the next day, my doodling habits seemed to be getting the better of me. I drew swirls and flowers about my notebook, no doubt the prettiest calculus notes anyone ever did see. My eyes left to look up at the board, the words of the professor entering in through one ear and out the other. Limits, limits, and more limits. Example after example filled the chalkboard, this professor obviously old school in their teaching style. I suppressed a sigh.

"If we wanna start on limits," I mouthed, covering my lips with my left hand as I returned to doodling with my right. "Let's talk about how you're totally crushing on your roommate's boyfriend."

I drew a squiggly heart then crossed it out. I exhaled with intent, tucked my hair behind my ears, and examined the chalkboard once more. But I couldn't focus. Never in my life had I fallen so quickly for a guy. Not that I had many chances. Maybe that's why my hormones were acting up.

Since leaving high school, I hadn't been on even one date. Even at the graduation parties held by my friends, I went and left alone. Maybe I was past due for a boyfriend. Or maybe I had finally found the one...

"Snap out of it."

I gripped my pencil as if trying to break it in half with the muscles of my palm. I prayed that it wouldn't snap though because plastic splintering skin was not pleasant.

My eyes found the board and I forced myself to listen to the teacher. Once I understood all I needed to from the lesson, I flipped ahead in my book to the practice problems and started running through them in my notebook.

"Hopefully some of these are the assigned ones, would really help free up time later for..." I paused. "Oh wait, I have absolutely no plans later because my life is super boring."

Working through some problems, I found ease at getting to the answer time and time again.

"Maybe math was my strong suit this whole time. Maybe I should switch majors."

I wanted a problem more challenging. The easier problems were allowing my mind to wander once more, as the muscle memory of writing line by line with basic arithmetic was too simple to keep me entirely occupied. My eyes scanned the page and landed on what looked like the perfect challenge.

Problem number 69.

I dropped my pencil and placed my palms to cover my eyes. That's it. I was too distracted to do this any longer.

The professor dismissed the class, writing the problems for our assignment on the board (with 69 not being one of them). I grabbed my belongings, shoved my notebooks quickly into my bag out of shame or embarrassment of someone noticing my doodles as they woke from their boredom, and jogged from the classroom.

My phone vibrated. I pulled it from my jacket pocket and noticed Jordyn texted.

Can you look at my precalc homework?? Don't need another C...

Whereas I loved math, she did not.

Another text came through.

Where r u??

I responded.

Heading to a techpod at the lab now. I'll see whats free and let you know

I walked outdoors to catch some fresh air. The day was clear, and the sun heated my skin the moment it touched me. The warmth distracted me from all else. I removed my earbud from my pocket and switched on an audiobook from my phone. Today was definitely a thriller kind of day.

The autumn air came with a breeze every now and again. A stray leaf that had decided to end its life cycle a tad earlier than the others would sweep across the path. School landscapers busied themselves in cutting the grass and trimming back trees, taking advantage of the beautiful day. I would have loved to do the same, but I still had two classes and a friend who needed a bit of tutoring.

I paused at the crosswalk, waiting for some light traffic to pass. As I looked across the way, my bouncing knees froze. Sara, Bridgette, and Chase sat in the grass under a tree in a small lawn outside the library. Bridgette braided Sara's hair and her and Chase sipped from their smoothies. I rolled my eyes, as I knew Sara's schedule enough to know she was missing a class to be there.

When my eyes came back around, they fell on Chase. Slivers of light shone through the obstruction of the tree canopy above them, hitting his face in the most flattering way. It shone to define every sharp angle of his face, every smooth muscle of his arms.

I shook my head and went to take a step forward. A car raced by, and I jumped back, forgetting where I was for a moment. My heart accelerated, now for two reasons. Looking both ways, despite the call of the void trying to convince me otherwise, I stepped to the crosswalk.

My thoughts swirled as I crossed the street. I debated turning up the volume of my audiobook but knew it would blow out my eardrums. My hearing was not something I wanted to mess with at my age.

"Just look at the ground, look to the sky, find something anything, but-"

I gazed in their direction. Chase stared at his phone while Sara and Bridgette laughed about whatever the gossip of the minute may be.

I stepped up on the curb. Having successfully crossed the road without killing myself, I refocused on getting to the computer lab. Just a couple of minutes away, I needed to get there and search out an empty pod for Jordyn and myself. If I didn't have one by the time she arrived, she would start sprinting about, ask the nearest group how long they thought they'd be before finishing, any number of oddities that most would be embarrassed about. And as her friend, I did tend to shy away whenever she did act out as so. It was who she was, and I accepted and loved her for it.

Even with the minor distraction, my curiosity itched, and I couldn't resist. With a slight, inconspicuous turn, I glanced at him. When my eyes found his, I realized he had already been looking at me. A relaxed grin formed on his face.

Turning away as quickly as I could, I picked up my pace and stared ahead, swearing I would not look back again.

I counted my steps and arrived at the lab by the time I reached step number 415 from the exact position from which I started counting. His brown eyes were so deep and rich I'm surprised I hadn't lost myself in that gaze. And his smoothie, it was definitely some variety of orange, which meant we had very similar tastes...

My phone vibrated. I expected it to be Jordyn, asking which pod I had grabbed. But I noticed it was just a notification to my social media. I opened up the app. It was a new friend request. I clicked the icon. My heart sank.

In the friend request tab, a picture of Chase and an account with his name appeared.

"It can't be the real him..."

I mumbled to myself, no longer concerned how crazy I may look to the other students. In fact, I came to the conclusion that most college students talk to themselves aloud with no concern or qualms whatsoever. And if their lives were even a pinch more exciting than mine, I was starting to understand why.

I clicked on the name which led to the account page. Sure enough, one of our mutual friends was none other than Sara, the rest of the group also appearing in his friends' group.

I sat on the nearest available couch, realizing that my slow pace was blocking others' travels. I couldn't wait to investigate, to know the truth. My heart was trying to escape my chest to think it could be real.

As I sat there scrolling through his feed, making sure it wasn't someone who possibly was just using his info, trying to befriend me then convince me to send hundreds of dollars in gift cards, a text comes through.

Where u at??

It was Jordyn.

"Shit..."

I stood and ran up the stairs, the updated study pods were on the second floor of the computer lab. I sprinted through the corridors and found an empty room.

208.

K

I sighed in relief. I placed my bag on the floor and took a seat. I pulled the provided laptop near and logged into my student account. My eyes kept moving to my phone, temptation growing.

As I crumpled to the pressure, Jordyn slammed into the door.

Ouch, she mouthed as she rubbed her head and reached for the handle. I shook my head and the laugh I tried to hold in came out like the sound of a raspberry. My face heated in the embarrassment, checking my phone screen to ensure I hadn't been recording or livestreaming myself to some feed he would be able to see. This paranoia to every little thing was surely the worst.

Jordyn slid the door back and popped into the pod. I stood and closed the door behind her, seeing she had no intention of doing so, for she was already digging through her bag for her notebook and laptop. Jordyn released a dramatic exhale.

"I swear," she started, huffing and puffing from her seated position. "There is absolutely no reason anyone should be holding their funeral in the local chapel. It's basically on campus and the entire procession took an eternity to pass. I would have been here a lot sooner, or maybe not. I swear I took off like a damn track star that forgot her uniform at home and brought her bag for some reason. I got some weird looks, but hey, I'm used to it."

She removed an energy drink from her bag, popped the tab, and swallowed near half of it before she came back up for air. She saw me on my phone and rolled her eyes.

"Are you going to help me, or are you busy?"

"I'm going to help, don't worry. I'm just... just a little distracted."

"From what happened last weekend?"

Her eyes grew wide, and she shook her head, as if expressing I need some sort of intervention. I sighed and issued a slight giggle.

"Maybe. Or maybe... hey. Do you have Chase as a friend on here?"

I showed her my phone, open to the tab of friend requests to show her his picture and name appearing. She was about to take another sip of her drink but instead harshly set down the can and bust out laughing.

"Oh. My. God. That's him alright. Yeah, I'm his friend. That's definitely him."

My face heated as I blushed. Excitement took my heart and my stomach as I thought about what this might mean. It could mean any number of things. He had been meaning to add me just because it's something to do on the app... He was thinking about me as he scrolled and recalled he had not yet sent me a request... He had been waiting for me to send a request but finally decided he could not take it any longer... It could be anything. But one thing was certain, he had in some way thought of me.

"Girl, I'm not going to get any of my homework done. Am I?"

We both started laughing. I crossed my arms and shrugged, a huge grin plastered across my face. With a shake of my head to bring me back to reality, I pulled out some dry erase markers from my bag and stood at the board.

"Okay, I'm ready. Give me the first one."

Jordyn shimmied her upper body as she flipped open her book. Her finger found the problem before her eyes, and she inhaled profoundly.

"Okay, umm." Jordyn examined the problem and sighed. She placed both hands on the desk and used it to push herself up. "I'm coming. This one comes with a picture."

I smiled and gazed out the glass panels on the one side of the pod, hoping to see that which would not pass. One who would not pass. He was probably still below, sitting in the grass. Sara and Bridgette were more than likely nonstop talking and somehow ignoring his existence. And Chase probably stared in the direction of the computer lab, tapping on his knee, waiting for an answer to the friend request.

But I didn't want to seem too eager. I didn't want to accept too fast. Keep him waiting. Keep him guessing. Keep him thinking of me. I wanted to stay on his mind the same as he was on my mind. I wanted to feel that he was suffering just as much as I was.

When we finished our lesson, which was more so me walking Jordyn through the problem as she nodded and jotted down my answer number for number, we headed to the food truck court for a quick snack. The area was surrounded by a small grassy lot with trees and picnic tables. Black squirrels ran about trying to collect any scraps the sparrows left behind.

"Taco truck, taco truck, taco truck," Jordyn sang as she ran for the taco truck.

Normally it was hit or miss what trucks set up in the court. But somehow, someway, the taco truck was always there when one most needed it.

"Hola," Jordyn mustered in her most American accent. The man at the window chuckled.

"Hola. What would you like?"

Jordyn tapped at her chin and examined the menu. I don't know why. She ordered the same thing every single time we stopped at this particular truck. But without fail, every single time we acted like it was precalc homework all over again.

"Carne asada with extra pico de gallo, please!"

I mouthed the words as she said them, nodding as the last of her order slipped from her mouth. The cook nodded and started frying some beef for her tacos. He looked to me and nodded his head, silently inquiring as to what I wanted.

"I'll take the same."

He shook his head to let me know he understood and added more beef to the grill. The smells hit just the spot on the beautiful autumn day.

I gazed about the park. Many students were relaxing on the grass, fast food boxes to one side, books on the other, intently typing at the phones in their hands. Others enjoyed their walks to class, some with headphones, some with friends. My eyes continued searching, as if the area in front of me was some I Spy book. I searched and searched but I didn't see him anywhere.

The man slid the white foam containers in our direction. I reached for my bag, but Jordyn held up her hand.

"I'm paying since you're tutoring me."

I wanted to question whether what I was doing was actually tutoring or just doing her homework for her. Either way, I was not turning down free tacos. Jordyn paid and we grabbed our food and headed for an empty picnic table.

The breeze brushed strands of hair across my face. I spit them from my mouth as I stepped over the wooden plank seat of the table. I straddled the plank for a moment, my bag trying to fall from my shoulder, placed my food on the table, and finally composed myself enough to sit properly. Jordyn ate as if her life depended on it, pouring as much pico de gallo as she could into her taco before gulping it down. A mix of tomato and onion juice slid from the corner of her mouth, a piece of cilantro stuck to her upper lip.

"You are such a mess," I joked and handed her a stack of napkins, never any less than a stack for tacos.

"I can't help it. I'm just as nervous as you."

"What do you mean?"

"While you were all wrapped up in boy drama, I saw news drop on The Lounge's page that they're having signups for a poetry night."

"That sounds right up your alley."

"Yea, it does. It's that, well, just thinking about it gets me all nervous and anxious and confused and-"

"If you're not ready then don't push yourself, there will be other times."

A disappointed look crossed her. Jordyn slouched over and took a hesitant bite of taco.

"I guess you're right. I'm just being dramatic."

I bit my lip, thinking I must have said the wrong thing. But I was just being rational. If you're not ready for something, just wait and build up the confidence until you are. Simple enough?

I eyed my phone, sticking from the side pocket of my bag. Was I ready?

I reached for my phone and opened up the app. His profile pic stared through me, waiting to see what I would do next. My finger hovered over accept. Fearing if I waited any longer that the request would disappear, I clicked it.

I turned off the screen and placed my phone screen down on the table. I opened up my box and sprinkled some pico de gallo into the tortilla.

And now I wait.

Chapter Three

My music blasted in my ears and my foot tapped along to the rhythm of the catchy beat. I never thought I'd like electronic dance music until I realized it was the ultimate study mode.

I typed out the conclusion for my group's chemistry lab write up, waiting for their comments as I typed but seeing none come through on our shared document. Without rolling my eyes, as I had learned to expect it by now, I closed by clearly stating the original hypothesis and how data collected was proof of its accuracy.

After typing the last word, I stared at the screen for several moments. A thumbs up from one group member came through. After a few seconds, I realized that was all I was going to get as confirmation. The assignment wasn't due until mid-morning the next day, so I would hold on sending in case anyone decided they did want to edit something. But I highly doubted that would happen.

With a simple goodbye, I closed that tab and skipped over to the one I had open as I searched for fall cardigans. My cursor scrolled and scrolled, hoping to find one that was highly rated but not as expensive. I gazed at the several cardigans Sara had draped over her bed's headboard. Money wasn't an issue for her, which explained the trash bags full of clothes that she still hadn't unpacked since she moved in. Unfortunately, impulsive buying was not something I could afford. I sighed.

Taking out my headphones, I listened closely for any movements in the hall or voices drawing near.

My attention returned to my computer. I pulled up my friends' page and clicked on his name. It took me to his profile, and I clicked immediately on the photos tab.

Scrolling through, I realized how little he posts pictures of himself. Most every photo from the past few months were uploads from his friends that he was tagged in. Granted the majority were from Sara. Pictures of them hugging, kissing, holding onto one another as if they were deeply fond of each other.

A pit fell into my stomach, and I closed the tab. I pushed out the chair and took a deep breath.

"You're being so stupid and desperate."

I gazed in the direction of Sara's bed and shook my head.

"Not just desperate but straight up obsessed. It's kind of creepy, actually."

As I stood, I noticed a pencil had dropped to the ground. I bent over to pick it up, and my phone vibrated on the desk. My entire body jumped, my thoughts distracting me from anything other than reality.

I picked up my phone and rolled my eyes.

Mom

I contorted my face in a way I'd be embarrassed for anyone to see. Hesitation crossed over me, hoping she had the wrong number. Clearly she wished to speak with my sister, getting our names mixed again. But the phone continued. As it neared vibrating off the corner of my desk, I reacted and answered.

"Hello?"

I wasn't sure why I always answered my cellphone like that. With the technology, I always knew who was calling. The better question to ask, rather than a revelation of identity would be "What do you want?" but that might be too abrasive.

"Hello, honey. It's your mother. How are you? How's school?"

"It's school. That's really it. Just studying, busy all the time."

Sitting down at my chair once more, I played with my pencil, rolling it between my fingers. My eyes scanned the room, trying to find any question but the obvious to ask next. She longed for me to ask how she was doing, and to do so would mean I'd be on the phone for the next hour as she spoke about how the divorce was going. I really didn't want to hear about all the horrible things my stepfather did for the hundredth time. I had already told her time and time again that he was just not a good person. She thought I was jealous of the attention she gave him rather than only giving attention to me. I could only ever roll my eyes.

Silence fell between us. She waited for it. My eyes landed on Sara's photo collage hanging above her desk, and I saw a picture of Chase in it. His eyes found me. My mind fluttered and I gave in.

"And how are you doing?"

My mom sighed in a mixture of relief and dramatic tone of "well let me tell you."

"I've been having just this massive struggle with this divorce..."

And then my mind drifted away. Thoughts of the horrible representation of marriage and relationships my mother had granted me caused me to feel a bit nauseous. Even if I ever did find myself in a relationship with a guy I would fall head over heels for, it would probably be doomed to a tragic end anyways. Granted, my father was doing much better now, and his girlfriend seemed like a pleasant person. But I didn't really talk to him much. Really only on the holidays, and only the ones which he decided to have my sister and I over. It was a no brainer deciding to go away for college.

"And he blames my lack of cooperation, saying he paid most of the bills. Pfft. I continue to work in this office so I can be home on time to cook his dinner, but he thinks him making more qualifies him for a greater percentage in the split. Well, I sent that denial straight back to his lawyer. We'll see what they draw up next."

And she kept going. Allegory after allegory to prove her point that she was the victim. Every now and again, she'd slip in a notice just to let me know that her current boyfriend is nothing like him, and equally as important to her that his credit limit is much higher.

I turned the phone on speaker and set it on my desk, deciding I could do other things while I listened to her going on. I pulled my basket of clean laundry up beside me and started folding.

In the middle of folding my cheeky underwear, the door flies open and Sara, Bridgette, and Chase file in. I threw my clothes in a rushed pile back into the basket, undoing any of the folding I had already done, and pushed it under my desk. With a rush, I jumped and turned my phone off speaker, a small sentence of warning about boys and "it will always end in divorce" left before I managed to do so. Expressions showed that the words had obviously met their ears.

"Ouch," Bridgette said, looking at me and in no way trying to hide her amusement. She jumped onto Sara's bed and withdrew her phone from her pocket.

"Mom, give me a sec."

I grabbed a jacket and walked for the door, blocked by Sara with arms out wide.

"Did you add my list to your order?"

"Yeah. It won't get here for a couple more hours. Excuse-"

Sara crossed her arms in an entitled rage.

"Seriously! You couldn't have-"

"Look, they might be backed up or whatever. I'm not calling to cause problems and then have them break all our eggs and send only rotten fruit."

"Then you call and leave a complaint."

"Then you do it. Excuse me."

"Whatever. I guess I can wait."

I glared as she continued to block the door. Chase placed his hands on her shoulders and pushed her inside. His eyes met mine and he attempted a smile as he passed.

"Thanks," I mumbled as I walked past and exited the room.

I turned as I heard the door latch behind me. I had hoped Chase left them in the room and followed me down to the study lounge. But he stayed with them.

"Okay, sorry about that, keep going."

And my mom happily did. I sat on the couch, people-watching and picking at my fingers as boredom and the desire to be elsewhere filled me. Not that I wanted to go back to my room. Not with them in there. I didn't want to hear Bridgette and Sara talk of how ugly or fat they were. I didn't want to see Sara hugging and kissing on Chase. I didn't want to slip up, to blush as our eyes met, to embarrass myself in front of him.

So, I sat there, giving reassuring sounds to my mother that I heard her, agreed with what she was saying, and everything else a supportive daughter should do.

"So have you met any boys?"

The question slipped in, and I was shocked as I hadn't been fully listening.

"Alex?"

"Well, yeah, I mean I've met tons of boys and girls and those who identify as-"

"Alexandria," her motherly tone slipped through, as if she were ready to nag me despite my age and being hundreds of miles away. "You know what I meant."

"Then no. I've just been focusing on my studies."

"You know your sister's already got one on the way, been with her man since high school. Wait too long and the good ones will be gone."

I didn't want to admit he already was.

"I just... I'm focusing on my classes. Once I start organic chemistry next semester, well, the difficulty is only going up from here."

"Suit yourself. But if you found a hard worker like your sister, you wouldn't even need to stress yourself out and go into massive debt at some school to prove yourself."

"I want a career, mom. Family will come with time. Or not. I'm young. I don't have to choose now."

"Oh, I hate hearing you say that." My mom's disappointed sigh almost blew out my ears as the echo-y whistle of quick releasing breath came. "At least I'll get grandkids from one of my daughters. Well, I should be getting off. A glass of wine has my name on it."

"Yep. Enjoy it."

"Take care. We'll talk soon. I love you, Alex."

"Yeah, love you, too."

I hung up my phone and leaned back on the sofa, head resting on the top of the cushion, staring at one of those ugly drop ceiling tiles above me. Of course, I should return and get my homework done, but I felt no desire to go back to my room. I sighed.

Sara and Chase had been together for two months, basically the day we moved into the dorms she came back that night, so excited she had met the "hottest man" on campus. We didn't really even know each other at the time. Her major of fashion merchandising would have no shared electives of mine in pharmacology. And despite our massive differences in upbringing, we managed to make our living arrangements work. She paid for most everything my food accounts wouldn't cover, and I kept the room clean and helped with her homework. I really didn't mind her as long as my earbuds didn't give out.

And I had seen them make out, cuddle, act grossly affectionate toward one another time and time again. Why did it bother me all of a sudden?

I could ask myself these stupid rhetorical questions all day. I knew why it bothered me. And I couldn't shake it. I couldn't return to that time before we kissed. It was like I was under a spell. Instead of the kiss waking me up, it sent me tumbling into a world of dreams with no escape.

Yet, I didn't want to wake up. Not yet. If anything, he was noticing me. And I craved that attention of recognition from him. Those subtle grins and locking eyes from afar may be enough to satisfy my racing heart for now. I just wondered how long it would take to turn from feeling affection to being tortured.

Chapter Four

S wirls and hearts, music notes and more hearts...
   My eyes scanned through the free elements available for use in our presentation.

A kissy mark, a soccer ball, another heart.

Even my computer worked against me.

"Ooh, click on that swirl!"

Jordyn pointed at my computer in excitement. It took a moment to see which icon she was talking about, the hearts seemingly sticking out and covering up any others around them.

I clicked and it appeared on our slide.

"It's cute, it is, but our project is about Phoenician influences in the ancient world."

"Yes, but it gives it that bit of style and pizzazz."

"I don't think pizzazz is going to give us extra points."

"Doesn't hurt to try."

I sighed and downsized the icon, leaving it in the corner. Jordyn nodded in approval, and we continued.

I never much liked group projects. At least Jordyn and I shared this one class that, out of all the classes, required at least one group presentation. Ancient Civilizations 101. An elective that somehow helped us to qualify for our degrees, though neither of us hoped to be historians in our future. Granted, Jordyn still hadn't really figured it out yet, so possibly possible.

I read through the text, flipping through slide after slide, adding cool transitions where necessary.

"Alright, now we just need to add some citations and we're good."

"To the internet!" Jordyn plugged in some quick web searches to pull up the most scholarly journals she could find.

"Actually, I was browsing the library's catalogue and noticed they had some great selections for this project."

"An actual book?"

"Yeah, I feel it will give our project that little extra something that additional swirlies and colorful elements won't."

I leaned back in my chair, observing her expression full of doubt and hesitation. Sara peeked at me from over her cellphone and returned to her own world after we made eye contact.

"Well, you go ahead and go. I'll stay and beautify these slides a little."

I stood and gestured to my laptop, letting her add her own personality to our assignment as I had micromanaged most up until that point.

"Oh, Alex," Sara called out, waving her hand in my direction. "If you're going out, can you pick up a strawberry, lemonade smoothie for me?"

"Ooh, good idea! I'll have a blueberry blitz!" Jordyn chimed in.

"And get an orange vanilla for Chase. He'll be over later."

I was going to say no until she brought up his name.

"Fine, who's paying."

Sara quickly held up cash, as if she had been begging me to stand up this whole time just to ask for that one thing.

"I'll let Chase know so he doesn't buy anything. You're the best!"

She sent an air kiss in my direction and rolled over into her blankets, legs in the air and kicking joyfully.

I pocketed the cash, grabbed a jacket, and headed for the library. I put in an earbud, popping on an audiobook I was so close to completing. Not many people were out and about. A brisk air rolled through campus in these evening hours, leaves gradually falling in higher and higher volume.

A skateboarder passed on my right, and I tipped my head in hello. As I brought my eyes back up from the ground, I saw a familiar form not far ahead. He sat on a bench outside the library and looked at his phone. Not even the cool air could cut through the warmth of my cheeks. I gulped as anxiety rose but decided I couldn't avoid it.

As I turned down the path to the library entrance, he stood and smiled at me, following me inside. My audiobook finished, an awkward silence filling my head. Do I take my earbud out? Do I let him keep thinking if he talks I won't be able to hear him? Can I even make any sudden moves, or will he assume I'm flirting with him?

I got in the elevator pressing the button for the third floor. Chase gestured for me to hold it, jumping in right alongside me. He smiled again, issuing a soft thanks under his breath.

I caught my breath, not wanting to breathe in the same space as him. Afraid that maybe being in close proximity to him is what caused me to fall in love so quickly. Perhaps it was a spell I was under and being so close to him may have been the key. It was no more than a few inches of space when we entered the closet. And when we kissed, that space disappeared, nothing between us.

He observed my face, wondering if he could talk. With a deep exhale, hoping to be brave, I removed my earbud. Relief shone in his eyes.

"How are you?" he asked, not even waiting for me to pocket the earbud.

I opened my mouth to answer but hesitated as the door opened and someone got in. We were already at the third floor. I panicked. Do I get off as I was supposed to do? Or do I stay on and carry on a conversation I would have only dreamed about the nights prior?

The door started to slide close, and I jumped. Chase reached a hand and prevented it from doing so.

"This was your floor, right?"

My face flushed in embarrassment. I nodded and exited the elevator. To increase that embarrassment, he walked out behind me.

"So, you're doing well?" he questioned again, not understanding how his proper grammar excited me, making me even more nervous to speak to him.

"Yeah," I nodded again, the only intelligible response I could give. "And you?"

I attempted the question despite the words coming out a bit choked. A tickle rose in my throat, but I refused to cough right here, right now.

"Yeah, I'm doing alright, thanks."

Our eyes connected and it sent my mind into a flurry.

"Did, uh, did Sara give you money for the drinks? She, uh, sent me a message, saying you were picking some up."

"Yeah," I replied, still trying to ignore the tickle in my throat but the feeling becoming unbearable.

He nodded and expressed and wide smile.

"Okay good, good. Well, I'll see you later, then."

I could no longer speak, so I committed to a friendly smile and wave. He tipped his head and reentered the elevator, almost colliding with another as he turned away to do so. He appeared slightly flustered and smiled back at me, his eyes failing to meet mine this time. I waved again and the door closed.

He was gone, descending back down the way we came. Did he only come up to ask me that? Did it worry him that Sara might not be paying? Or did he just want a reason to talk to me?

I rushed to the ancient civilization texts and coughed up a storm as my throat's bothersome irritation caught up to me. My eyes watered and I tried my best to ignore the eyes looking in my direction, ensuring I wouldn't die among the stacks. I saw a librarian at a desk clutching her hand sanitizer near.

With as much urgency as I could, I found the books, checked out, and made for the dorms, almost forgetting the smoothies along the way.

I stepped very carefully as I entered our room, not wanting even the tiniest drip to crawl over the plastic dome lid of his cup. I set down the cardboard cup holder and dropped Sara's change on her desk. She was no longer in the room, Jordyn sitting in silence and darkness on my computer.

"You can turn on a light, you know."

I pulled the metal cord for my desk lamp, and it lit up the space in a blinding flash. Jordyn jumped back, as if a vampire about to accidentally walk into the sun.

"The computer's light was just enough."

I shook my head.

"And you wonder why you need glasses. Your eyes can't focus well in the dark, so stop trying to force them to."

"I don't think your science checks out."

I shrugged and passed her the smoothie blend she had asked for. She took a long slurp from the straw and let out a sound of satisfaction.

"That hit the spot."

We continued to work on our project into the night. I flipped to random pages in the book that we could cite in our presentation, hopefully convincing even if just the professor that we did thorough research of the subject.

The doorknob wiggled and came flying open as Sara and Chase entered. Sara was already obnoxiously laughing from seemingly the funniest joke in the world. Chase's face read as if he hadn't said anything amusing nor comical in the slightest.

"Oh, you got our drinks! You're such a doll." She put on a fake Jersey accent, reminding me of a trip through Queens when I had decided to check out the city as I passed through to get to this university. But I was no expert on accents, just as she was no professional actress anyways.

"Thanks!" Chase smiled and went to grab his smoothie. He hesitated. "Which one is mine?"

"Oh, sorry," I jumped up in a panic and looked at the x's on the side of the cup. "That one. This is orange, vanilla, and cinnamon. It's mine."

"Cinnamon? Interesting. I might have to try that sometime."

My heart skipped a beat, and I strolled back to my bed, smoothie in hand. My hands trembled from the nerves, so I decided to place the cup on the desk until I was ready for it, or in the least able to control my muscles from spasming.

Jordyn and I added effects to the presentation, Jordyn still at the helm as she was the more creative one. And luckily she didn't mind this part because I kept getting distracted. Chase and Sara sat on her bed, backs against the wall and stared at their phones. Every once in a while, he would say something to try to start up a conversation with her. Sara would answer with no more than a brief response and turn her attention away once more.

Jordyn and I finished up, pleased with the final result. With a huge yawn, Jordyn grabbed her things, waved goodbye, and headed back to her dorm. Now it was just the three of us.

Retrieving my earbud from my pocket, I decided the best way to pass the time was to start a new book. But I only chose to block one ear, curious as to any conversation that might still transpire.

About fifteen minutes passed and Chase stood. He stretched at the side of Sara's bed, the lamp light hitting his muscles in all the right ways, leaving little to the imagination. As his arms reached over his head, Sara lunged and wrapped her arms about his waist. My eyes quickly moved to my comforter.

"Do you think you could take me to Mimi's tomorrow to get my nails done?"

Chase abandoned his stretch and unwrapped her arms from around him. He sat on the edge of her bed.

"You know I have practice tomorrow. Or do you not have the schedule?"

"I might have lost it…"

Sara expressed a pouty face that a child feigning innocence may wear. I couldn't decide whether I wanted to puke or laugh.

"Typical." He shook his head and stood.

"So, can you take me?"

"Did you not hear me? I have practice tomorrow."

"Seriously? You can't give up one day of practice to take me?"

"What? And have them kick me from the team and lose my scholarship? I don't think so. Ask Bridgette."

"But she has an evening class tomorrow."

Sara rolled around on her back, kicking her legs in the air in some weird form of a tantrum. She stopped and sat up as a thought struck her. Fluffing her pillow, she threw it at my face. Luckily, I had been paying enough attention to stop it in time.

"What was that for?"

"Since Chase is being a dummy, you have to take me to get my nails done tomorrow. Because at least you actually care about me."

She stuck out her tongue at Chase, trying to rub his loss in his face. As if any moment not spent with her would torture him.

"I can't."

"What?"

"I'm busy."

Sara crossed her arms and turned from us both. Chase's eyes met mine, shining in his victory. He messied the hair atop Sara's head, her arms waving like an angry squid to prevent him touching her. A playful grin found me, and he winked.

"Thanks again."

He lifted his smoothie and walked out the door.

Chapter Five

While my professor droned on about the carbon atom and the miraculous way in which it bonds, I peered out the window, lost in my own world. Robins hopped about searching for worms, squirrels ran up trees with puffed up cheeks. Temperatures were steadily rising again this week, a few days of no-jacket-needed exciting all on campus.

My lab partners were on their phones, also not caring to listen to the professor's enthusiasm for the subject. Picture after picture covered the whiteboard. Without context, none of them would make any sense. Atoms and arrows all over the place and pointing every which way. There was no saving me from boredom now. Even if I wanted to, I would never be able to find my place back into this discussion having zoned out for so long.

Lucky for me, chemistry was not a sore subject. I thoroughly enjoyed it more than biology, which felt like an absolute drag as I learned the same things covered in my high school class three years ago. Perhaps it would pick up at some point, but probably not this semester.

Everyone always freaked out about freshman year, but it didn't seem so bad. Classes were going well, I already got used to the dorm lifestyle. Maybe it's because I learned to be self-sufficient back home, doing the shopping and chores, cooking quick meals so I could get out of the house as soon as possible to spend time at Jordyn's place. Her parents were always so welcoming, her house my second home.

As autumn passed by, I remembered the retreats we would have, running to her house after school for hot chocolate and marshmallows. It was our snack and our dinner. Her mom would scold us in the most caring way, eyes warning to hide it from my mom. The one thing she never realized is that my mom wouldn't care anyways. It was enough for my stepdad and her that I was out of the house, out of the way, and not a bother to the lifestyle they wanted to live.

I grabbed a highlighter and reviewed the day's notes. I highlighted any key terms or concepts to ensure easier studying. The professor circled back around, finally, to the original question asked by the student, at which point I tuned back in, hoping to learn something new.

At long last, the professor reminded us of our online assignment and dismissed the class. Most every other student had readied at least five minutes ago, racing to the door once permitted to do so. I took my time gathering my things, not wanting to battle with the traffic.

"Have a good rest of your day, Alex," Mr. Boyce waved to me, as I was the last headed out the door.

"You as well." I smiled and returned the wave. He stood at the board, gazing with pride upon his beautiful artwork covering it. A grin crossed his face.

Once in the corridor, I headed for a small grouping of tables and seats. Most of the tables were empty, the good weather outside and time of day both significant factors. It was midafternoon, most done with their classes for the day and either headed to extracurriculars or to any other number of things to do around campus with their friends.

My phone vibrated, and I pulled it out, curious as to who it could be.

Nails? (crying face emoji)

Sara. I released a breathy giggle and replied.

Sorry. Busy right now.

I checked the time.

"They should have started already," I mumbled.

I left the science building and walked the path outside. I checked the first field and noticed the women's soccer team practicing there. Disappointment crossed my face as I realized the men's team must be at the other field. I picked up my pace and hoped to make it before their practice ended. Not that it would take long to get there, I was just being a bit dramatic in my thinking. But I couldn't stop myself from always thinking of the worst possible scenario.

The smell of fresh fries caught me as I passed a food truck. Deciding I couldn't ignore my grumbling stomach, and not knowing how much time I would be spending at the field, I bought a small box and continued on my journey.

When I finally arrived, I saw all the guys on the field running a couple of drills. I didn't know much about soccer, having never played or watched a live game in my life. The only time I ever even cared was the Olympics a few years back, and that was only because the women's team made it pretty far into the bracket. Everyone else seemed to care, so I just followed along with it so I could participate in the conversations as well.

I found a seat in the bleachers at the side of the field and set my bag down. I studied my phone for a bit, looking up every now and again to watch the team. And then the sun hit just right, and I saw him. Chase tossed his head, trying to force aside the loose hairs that fell in front of his face.

My phone vibrated. I jumped, not realizing I had been staring for possible minutes at him. I checked the screen to see a snippet of the message. It was no more than a crying face emoji again from Sara. I rolled my eyes and put my phone down at my side, ignoring the message.

I withdrew my notebook and my math book from my bag, getting some homework done outdoors on this beautiful day enough of an excuse to give to my roommate later. Every once in a while, I looked up, watching his athletic form jog across the field, passing the ball from one person to another. Though many of the guys on the team were quite attractive, none compared to him.

The team broke into two to do a scrimmage, practicing their plays amongst themselves. My interest grew to see actual playing. Chase huddled with his team, and they jogged to their positions. My stomach fell. He was headed this way.

He watched the ground as he moved toward my side of the field. When he finally looked up, his eyes caught mine and a surprised smile formed on his face. His hand rose, as if to wave, but then moved to push his hair back, moving the strands once more from his eyes.

I returned a smile and waved. With both hands, I gestured a thumbs up, wishing his side good luck. He nodded in thanks but didn't look away. His eyes kept watch over me, examining to check that I was truly alone, no one else was with me. Checking perhaps that no one else would see. Distracted by his thoughts, he missed the kickoff.

My face changed and my hands urged him to get back to the scrimmage. I reached for my french fries and slowly chewed on every greasy stick, enjoying both the salty taste and the view.

His eyes continued to find mine, his own sparkling as the sun hit him just right. Sweat glistened on his forehead as he gave his all, running for the ball between passes, trying to get it away from the opposing team. He attempted a goal many times, hitting goalposts or the goalie catching them with his every attempt. He threw his hands up to his head, yelling a curse that couldn't be heard over the excitement of the rest of the team.

Soccer may not be for me, or maybe it was growing on me, but either way, I could not say the game didn't interest me. Time was running out on the clock, their scrimmage mimicking a real game's playtime.

Chase waved an arm in the air, reminding his teammate that he was open, there was space to pass the ball. He ran back and forth to avoid his blocker getting too close. As he zoomed in toward the opposing team's goal, he shouted. His teammate passed the ball and Chase kicked it straight past the goalie's leg. The ball hit the back of the net, and everyone roared in excitement. I threw my box of fries to the side and applauded the goal.

Chase screamed and hugged his teammates flooding toward him for an embrace. When they released, they all jogged back for the kickoff. Chase looked to me and pointed. My heart accelerated.

From everything I knew about sports, when one scores and points to a person or to the skies, it means 'that was for you.' I stopped clapping in an instant and stood there in shock. My mouth agape, any to look upon me may have thought the fries were not sitting well in my stomach. And maybe they were right. Greasy food did not mix well with the flying butterflies.

I sat and grabbed the box of French fries. Though I had no intention to eat any more, I needed to distract myself with something. My face flushed and I fanned at my cheeks, the heat of the day no competition to my internal body temperature. If I was truly trying to forget about this creepy crush, his every action did not help.

The game ended, his goal being the one they needed to put them over the top and clutch the victory. His teammates took a break and gathered for hydration about the jugs of sport drink where they had all of their other things scattered across the ground.

I had found distraction in my phone and hadn't realized he jogged in my direction until I heard my name.

"Alex, hey."

Chase slowed to a walk and wiped any residual sweat from his face. He took a gulp from his water bottle and smiled at me in a way that forced his eyes to close slightly. Genuine happiness.

"Hi," I responded, feeling like I owed him at least that much.

"I've never seen you interested in sports before. Why'd you decide to stop by?"

His glittering eyes begged for the answer that was probably the most honest response. But to provide the most honest response would reveal just how creepy I was. *Well of course I'm stalking you and watching and following you to your activities...* That wasn't exactly the flirtatious answer I'd hoped it could be.

"Well, it's a beautiful day and I just needed some fresh air. Figured I could sit down here and just watch, I guess."

He laughed and took a seat on the bleacher at my side. He was so near I could have reached out and touched him. His chest puffed up and down rapidly due to still trying to catch his breath. He grabbed at his stomach and let out a groan.

"Man, I am so hungry."

I held up my box of fries to offer to him.

"Sorry, it's all I've got."

"Seriously?"

He hesitated but decided to take one and eat it. He made a satisfied moan. My eyes averted to the ground, not wishing my emotions to get the better of me.

"I've always loved these. He makes them just right."

Chase stood up and stretched his legs, holding his foot up behind him one after another. He tried to catch my eyes, which still looked to the dirt, examining an ant trying to carry a leaf to its home. His head tilted and he slowly bent over until I turned to him.

"Actually, I was wondering if you wanted to get a bite to eat. You know, to celebrate that awesome goal."

My stomach sank. I would never be able to eat a french fry again. I felt like Chase knew he was singlehandedly ruining everything for me, as everything I enjoyed was starting to remind me of him. And he was still the guy who was my roommate's boyfriend. Not single. Not available. My biggest mistake was caving to their stupid game.

Realizing my cue, I slid my math textbook and notebook back into my bag. I shook my head, surely something I would regret later, but I felt neither option was good.

"I- I can't."

His jaw dropped and he scratched at his side.

"Oh, did I-"

"No." I shook my hands frantically in front of me and brought them to my mouth while I formulated my response. "I just- I don't think Sara would-"

At saying her name, Chase released an agitated exhale and turned to his team, checking that they were still on break.

"Listen, it's just some food. If she reads into it, that's on her."

I squeezed my lips shut, not wanting to argue with him. He knew as well as I did what her response would be. He seemingly didn't care either way.

"And honestly, if she really cared, she would have been here to see that goal, and I would have taken her instead."

So, he was comparing this to a date in some way. Suggesting I was taking the spot of his unsupportive girlfriend, like a fill in for someone who should care, I felt even worse about accepting his offer. But I did.

"Okay. Okay let's-"

His face changed in an instant. Relief found his eyes and he glanced back to see the team was lining up for more drills on the field.

"Alright, cool, yeah." He scratched at his head as he started to walk backwards. "Just like fifteen minutes left of practice and then we'll, uh. Well, I have to get a change of clothes, and then we'll..."

"Take your time," I smiled. My stomach relaxed after much anxiety, to think I would finally have the chance to sit and talk with him, just us once more.

His facial expressions softened. He waved goodbye for now and joined his team.

I leaned forward, elbows on knees and head in hands.

"What am I getting myself into?"

My phone vibrated.

I've got this awesome idea for a poem for poetry night, but I need some help. Can you come over asap?

Jordyn.

A chill coursed up my spine as a breeze struck through the shadow casted on me by the changing position of the sun in the sky. Endless drama was bound to hit with all my current decisions. Regret wouldn't be too far behind.

The last drill ended, and the team snacked, hydrated, and grabbed their bags as they scattered in all directions. Chase waved at me from the far end of the field, a gesture to wait as he gathered his belongings. I motioned back that I understood.

My phone gripped tight in my hand, I sent the only response I could.

Sorry. Busy right now.

Chapter Six

C hase and I passed by his dorm on the way to a local dine in. He got a change of clothes and even washed up a bit, the smell of after shave catching me off guard with his return.

"I'll carry that for you."

He pointed at my backpack. I laughed and shook my head.

"Don't be ridiculous."

"We didn't even stop by your room to drop it off. I'm the one who invited. It's the least I can do."

"We didn't stop by the room because Sara is probably pouting and would have an unlimited number of questions preventing me from leaving for the rest of the night."

Chase chuckled and rubbed the back of his neck, understanding the truth I spoke.

"Are you sure?" he inquired again, moving closer as if he would take it anyways.

"I'm good, thanks."

He backed off. Silence fell between us as we walked. A breeze coursed through campus as the low temperatures of the evening threatened an awful end to a beautiful day. Crisped leaves skirted across the path in front of us, crunching under our feet as we went.

My phone vibrated nonstop, but I ignored it. My hand itched to reach for it, but I wanted to keep my hands free, unoccupied, just in case something else might find their way into them.

Chase's hands were tucked into a jacket he had grabbed when changing, though it didn't hide the fact that his fingers were fidgeting within the pockets. The corner of my mouth raised as I noticed, wondering if he was really as nervous as I was. It was odd to me. He was dating a woman much more beautiful than me. Was he nervous because he found me attractive as well? Or was he worried about getting caught?

We arrived at the dine in, smells of cheeseburgers and fries swirling about the air and causing my stomach more grumbling than it already threatened. Chase opened the door and stepped to the side. I glanced at him, a grin forcing its way on my face, my fingers finding my hair and pulling at my split ends. He returned a gentle grin and followed me in.

After being led to a table, Chase fought to get past me again, presumably to pull my chair out, but I had already done so, not having thought about it. He jerked back as he realized he was too late to do so and reversed back to his seat. The server dropped our menus and gave Chase a lingering gaze as she walked away. An odd jealousy hit that was entirely unjustified.

"So, that was a nice goal, right?"

He kept going back to that. It was as if he longed to get approval from someone, anyone. Perhaps it was the only reason he invited me out. I was a witness to his amazing skills, those which got him a scholarship in the first place. He had no doubt been praised in his high school days, but that wasn't the case now. College sports were a different level of skill. Only the best from all over the country competed. Many of his friends, once top of their teams, would never make it on the college field. He needed approval, to erase the doubts that it wasn't some mistake that he had received the scholarship. He needed to know that he was worth it.

I hadn't seen this self-conscious side of him. He expressed a vulnerability I hadn't realized he possessed. But that weakness, it made him more human. It cut at my nerves, an understanding that he wasn't some perfect, supermodel being that had it all figured out. And perhaps my obvious imperfections made him more comfortable, more relaxed.

"It was great," I giggled. I played with the silverware in front of me, unraveling the napkin from the spoon and fork and laying it on my lap. I distracted myself in spreading it like a blanket over my thighs, hiding my face as I smoothed every wrinkle. My heart hadn't stopped racing since his acknowledgment of my existence on the field. My brain threatened to shut down, but I fought. I had to.

"It means a lot. That you were there to support me."

My head shot up from my lap, my eyebrows furrowed in confusion.

"I mean," Chase stumbled over his words. "I mean that you were there to see that. That goal. That you saw since you were there. It's... It was... cool."

His eyes landed on my face, and I swore they had focused in on my lips. My gaze turned to the server who brought our drinks, nodding in thanks. I forced a smile, but it almost betrayed me and turned to a frown. With his anxious energy, my heart and stomach would never calm.

"Can I take your orders?" the server asked, not even bothering to pull out a pad of paper.

Chase peered at me, signing to go ahead and order first.

"Ah, I'll just have a slice of cheese pizza."

"Same," he said, not a second after I finished.

"Okay, two slices of cheese. Anything else?"

We both shook our heads. The server nodded and walked away.

"You're nervous, aren't you?" Chase asked, his volume at little more than a whisper.

"Well, I mean, it's not like I don't know you're dating someone. This just feels... I don't know... a bit dirty?"

Chase licked his lips and gazed at the table.

"I'm sorry to put you into this sort of predicament."

"I mean, I could have said no."

"You're too nice. I knew you wouldn't say no."

He leaned back in his chair and crossed his arms.

"I guess I should be nervous too, but I'm really not."

He leaned forward and put both hands on the table. I questioned in my head that if I'd had my hands anywhere near if he would have grabbed them.

"It's complicated, and I guess I shouldn't speak bad of Sara in front of you, it's just..."

His eyes found mine, my mind possibly playing tricks as I thought I read sadness in him. His mouth hung open, no more words forming. The only sound being the other conversations playing in the background of the diner. Other couples laughed, friends talking in high pitched voices as they joked with one another. Our table held a different energy. Serious.

"Things are complicated right now."

He sighed and resigned from the conversation. Our pizza arrived. The server eyed us both, glaring at me as if I had said something to bother Chase. She dragged a finger along his side of the table after placing his plate, as if hoping to grab his attention. It didn't work as she had planned. With pursed lips, she returned to her job.

"I do want to say," he perked up at the sound of my voice. "I've never really watched a true soccer game, but you did a great job out there." He grinned. "I mean, truly, you have great condition."

His smile grew, and I almost gulped as I thought about what could be assumed from my compliment. Even now I could make out a toned core under his shirt, which fit a bit snug but perhaps that how he liked it. Maybe it's the only reason he removed his jacket anyways.

"So, Sara has never gone to one of your practices?"

I tried to strike up an actual conversation he could participate in. For some stupid reason, I chose a topic that would only serve to increase his resentment of his girlfriend, my roommate. It felt like an underhanded tactic. As if trying to win him over by trashing their relationship. But that wasn't really the case. I was curious. It seemed odd as she was almost never in the room. And I could have sworn I heard her talking about watching someone's practice, I just assumed it was his.

"Not one."

His expression didn't spell anger, but it was more playful. As if understanding my blatant confusion and wanting to set the record straight.

"What about your games? Any of those?"

"She said she has, but I honestly don't remember ever seeing her in the stands. Not sure what I expected. That she'd be sitting out there with a sign or shirt with my name on it, I don't know. Some of the other guys have ladies that do that for them, some not even in relationships, just like admirers."

"And you don't have any admirers?"

He laughed and shook his head, biting his lip in a flirtatious way. My heart leapt but I knew I couldn't break eye contact with him now.

"No, I don't think so. Unless you know something I don't."

And there went my appetite. My tossing stomach would never allow me to eat now.

"I... I don't think I can answer that. After all, we haven't really hung out a whole lot."

"And yet you seem to be everywhere."

So, he noticed, too.

"Look, I don't know where tomorrow will take us. Just know that I've really enjoyed this."

He smiled and took a bite of his pizza, pointing to it as he does so to express his joy of the taste. I giggled and decided I might as well eat. Even if the tsunami in my stomach wouldn't calm, I'd have to get used to the storm for a while. Or at least I wanted to try.

The bill came and he snatched it up before I could take a look. Not that we ate much, but I still wanted to put forth my share.

"No, no, no," he shook his finger and removed a card from his wallet. "I've got this."

"Despite what Sara may say about me, I can pay for my own things."

"I always take what she says with a grain of salt anyways. No, I invited you here."

I sat back and folded my arms, wanting to exert my stubborn pride but trying to enjoy the moment. My phone vibrated as I started to zone out, bringing me back to reality.

I peeked and noticed loads of missed texts from Jordyn, asking when I'd be available, what I was doing, why I wasn't answering. If I told her the truth, she would say I'm a traitor and give me the silent treatment for weeks, which didn't seem like that big a deal.

The server returned his card after payment, and I stood from my seat, anticipating walking back to the dorm alone. He didn't move, watching me as I adjusted my shirt, trying to move the fabric from emphasizing my bloated stomach. I exhaled and looked everywhere but at him directly.

"I meant what I said, you know. This has been nice."

"Yeah," I nodded, still refusing to make eye contact. "Thanks for the invite. It's been nice hanging out as friends."

He chuckled and tossed his hair to the side.

"Yeah. Yeah."

"I gotta head back before it gets too dark."

Chase stood and zipped up his jacket.

"Let's head out."

Chase reached out his hand, muscle memory taking over. I stared at him, my eyes moving from his hand to his face. He shook his head and clenched his fist as he pulled it back to his side.

"I'm sorry. That was not... I clearly wasn't thinking straight."

Silence fell between us. He led the way out and I followed behind, leaving a bit of distance in doing so.

As he said he would, he walked me to the door of the dorm building. With no more than a wave, he departed, kicking at the dried leaves gliding across the pavement.

As I ascended the stairs, I read through my missed texts. My stomach grumbled as I debated how to best answer them, with honesty or white lies. I knew if I chose the latter, I would soon be entangled in a web I may never be free of. And yet, honesty would lead me down the same path.

The only thing I could do was hide the truth. I wouldn't have to fear Chase telling anyone, of that I was positive.

Chapter Seven

The weight of my calculus book was useless if it didn't help my arms slim as I pumped it over my head. As I bench pressed the book, up, down, up, down, I kicked at the air, moving my feet as if riding a bicycle. I thought about his toned legs, his muscular arms, the way his abs pushed against his form-fitted shirts. Just the thought of all the greasy foods I ate yesterday kept me going, knowing if it became a common occurrence, I would need something to counteract the effect on my body. And secretly I prayed it would keep happening.

I read the text as I brought it near and then pushed it away from my face. Exercising had to double as studying, for I didn't have time to do both independently of the other. Slipping on my grades was something I refused to do for a boy, even if that boy was a man.

A loud thud ran into the door. Startled, my book fell on my face, and I jumped from my bed, wiping sweat from my chest with my shirt. A jingling of keys occurred, then Sara thrust open the door in a fit of rage, tears streaming down her face. She slammed the door and faceplanted into a pile of pillows she had on her bed.

Crying, a grief of one losing someone super close was the only way I could think to describe it. I had never seen anyone so broken in my life until this point.

Biting down on my lip, I watched her concern, wondering if I should say something, wondering if she just needed some alone time. After a quick thought, I realized she definitely wanted to talk about it. That was her coping style. Any drama, any anger, anything that caused her to have an emotional response, she liked to talk about it. I wasn't sure I was the one to offer my shoulder for her to cry on.

I sighed and stepped over to her bed, sitting down on the edge.

"What's up? What's wrong?"

Sara unburied her face from the pillows for a moment to look at me. Her eyeliner and mascara caused dark circles to form about her eyes, accentuating the sadness her expression brought. With her eyes full of tears, I had to look away, quickly regretting all that had transpired the day before.

She wiped her tears and any escaping mucus on her blanket. Taking a few calming breaths before diving in.

"He... somehow, he found out. And now... he was screaming at me. Saying I didn't care."

She spoke between a trembling voice and sporadic arm movements. I couldn't quite piece together the puzzle, but it seemed to be the opposite of what I was expecting.

"You know I don't know what you're talking about. Take it back a bit. He? You mean Chase? What did he find out?"

Sara grabbed a pack of moistened wipes from her desk and dabbed under her eyes. She licked her lips and crossed her legs as she sat with a pillow on her lap.

"So, one of the guys from the football team just started talking to me out of nowhere at one of their practices, and we just kept talking after that. And, well, I ended up, maybe just like a few times, hanging out with him. But it was just like friends."

She waved her hands in front of her, as if assuming where my head was going and trying to redirect my thoughts. The irony, if only she knew.

Sara played with the hair draped over her shoulder, fidgeting with the strands and furrowing her brow at every found split end.

"And you never told Chase about this friend?"

"Well, no. I knew he would get all jealous. He always acts so entitled."

I gulped, as if I should take her warning and run myself while I still could. I sighed.

"Well, can't you just apologize? Swear you'll never see this other guy again?"

Sara looked at me with yearning eyes, an expression that read she was the victim, that she had done nothing wrong.

"But... I guess that might be the only way. But... he also can't just yell at me like that. It was totally uncalled for, and I don't know how I could ever look at him the same again."

Her phone rang. She picked it up, wasting no time in doing so, and threw it in my direction after seeing the picture. We both sat in silence until the ringing stopped.

"Who does he even think he is?"

Her phone dinged as a message came through.

"What does it say?"

Sara stared at me. Getting involved in their drama was definitely something I'd regret later. If not for the guilt already eating at my insides, I probably would have just walked away. I picked up her phone.

Can we talk?

I read it out loud to Sara as another came through.

We can still work this out.

My heart plummeted. Stomaching my emotions, my eyes found hers.

"Do you want to respond?"

Sara pursed her lips, and a satisfied grin passed her expression before shaking her head.

"Just say like, 'Oh, so you wanna talk now?'"

I opened up the message, noticing the previous day's good night text with hearts and other emojis. I took a deep breath and wrote exactly as she spoke it. My finger hovered over the send button, forcing my eyes closed in order to do so. The "L" word was there. My stomach grumbled.

"You do realize you don't even have a lock screen set up, right? I just got straight through to your messages."

"Oh. My. God." Sara clutched a pillow to her chest, her fingers digging in like claws. "That son of a bitch. He must have read my messages when I forgot my phone in his room. That's how he knows."

"You forgot your phone? When was this?"

"This past weekend. He must have known since then and was just waiting to see if I was going to admit something to him."

My heart almost stopped, the vibration of the phone in my hand like the shock I needed to start it back up again. But I didn't want to look. If I read his response, surely I would feel so far detached from reality that I would never find my way back.

"Well? What did he say?"

I inhaled a shaky breath and found at least the semblance of courage to form words and spoke them aloud.

I was stupid. Please. Let's work through this.

Sara scoffed and rolled around in her bed. An excited cackle, starting low then bursting with volume echoed off our walls. She started singing "I've got him wrapped around my finger..."

"Ah, this is cute now, isn't it? Tell him sure. Come over here and we'll work through it. I would say to also add a winky face, but I don't want to make it too awkward for you. And anyways, I want him to beg for it."

I sent the message and promptly handed her the phone. I left her bedside, drifting slowly yet steadily over to mine. I felt like a ghost. I had been so dumb and naïve. I knew it. I knew it. The same paranoid thoughts from when this all started swirled in my head and I internally screamed at not seeing the signs sooner.

"Sorry to do this, but when he gets here, can you head out for a bit? If we're gonna make up, then... well... I shouldn't have to tell you, you're old enough to know."

"Sure thing," I mumbled, not knowing what else I could possibly say. But she was right in her thinking. When he got here, I wanted to get as far away as possible.

I slid my textbook into my backpack and put my notebook beside it. After zipping it up, I couldn't do anything other than just sit for a moment, still processing everything that flew through my mind. I stared at my phone, wondering what I was waiting for.

There was a knock at the door.

Sara cleared her throat, a not-so-subtle indication that she wanted me to answer.

I swung my backpack around my shoulder and, with quickened pace, opened the door.

Wide eyes found me, though I avoided looking at him. I couldn't, now and maybe not ever again, see him in the same way.

His hand reached for the back of his head, grabbing at his hair and not able to form any words even as his mouth opened.

"Don't worry. She was just leaving."

His mouth closed and his eyes turned to the ground.

"Yeah. Don't worry. I'm leaving. Don't want to ruin the fun."

Chase's head darted up, squinted eyes and parted lips demonstrating confusion. I tried to convince myself that he's playing me for dumb, this is how he manipulates. My stomach dropped and a feeling of needing the bathroom hit.

I pushed past to get out of the room and jogged to the lobby below.

Not many students were around, so I had my pick of seat. The L-sofa called to me, as I felt that may be my sleeping arrangements for the night. To say students slept and napped in the lounges at times would be an understatement. In fact, the lounges were probably cleaner than most of their rooms. Not to mention, the dorms were rife with drama, drug and alcohol experimentation, and freshman who only attended to get the chance to leave their home life behind. It wasn't much different for me. It was an escape. But it was also an opportunity. And if I kept getting distracted, going back to the life I thought I had left behind may be the only way to survive.

I removed my shoes and curled up on the sofa. My backpack taunted me, asking me why I even brought it in the first place if I had no mind for studying anyways. I ignored it and stared at the ceiling, citing formulas to ensure they were fully memorized. I repeated the formulas for hyperbolic functions over and over.

"D over dx of sine h of x is equal to cosine h of x."

I kept going over and over. Tears formed but I swallowed back my emotions. My phone tempted me from my peripheral vision. *Call Jordyn. Ask for a shoulder to cry on.* But I couldn't. If I just fought the feelings time and again, eventually I would get over the desire to cry. I would get over him.

My eyelids closed, exhaustion taking me. The lights glowed red when my eyes closed completely. I didn't care to be sleeping in the light rather than complete darkness. Caring about any discomfort was not even worth giving thought.

I awoke a few hours later. I expected a chill to hit in the dead of night, but noticed a jacket covered my legs, which had curled up to my chest. It had the familiar smell of aftershave.

I buried my head in my hands, unable to stop the tears now.

Chapter Eight

I had managed to wander up to my bed in the night, though I still awoke the next morning with a cramped neck and eyes that yelled at me for opening them. Sara slept, almost unseen among the hill of pillows and the blankets she used in addition to her comforter. The energy of the room was too still, the halls too quiet. Granted, Fridays always tended to be the days of worst attendance around here.

As I kicked my legs over my bed, I noticed the jacket sleeve sticking out from under it. I tucked it back into hiding, not wishing for Sara to see. I didn't want to forget about it, but I also could not stomach seeing it myself.

I sat there, on the edge of my bedding, feeling like every second I was sliding off. My feet planted themselves on the ground, so I didn't risk actually falling. But I knew the surprise caused by the sensation, throwing me off balance, would result in me landing hands and knees on the floor. It was one of those things. I could prepare and anticipate the fall, but, when the time came, it all would have been for nothing.

The clock on my phone faded in and out. Little icons appeared to show I had missed messages and calls. Jordyn's list of misses was longer than any other. I took a deep breath, and without reading through the chain, replied.

I'm so sorry. We'll catch up today.

Hoping Jordyn was still sleeping and that she wouldn't see my message right away, I packed a quick snack, grabbed my bag, and headed out.

Fresh, autumn air smacked me in the face as I left the dorms. A chill that stung my nose and forced a shiver up my spine, yet was a comfort as I crossed my arms tighter across my chest to feel warmth, welcomed me.

It woke me up, thank goodness, because drowsiness was the last thing I wanted to feel today.

My first class was calculus, and it was an exam day. I couldn't allow any feelings to distract me. It wasn't worth it. I had to maintain my grades or be forced to question everything I was putting on the line to be here. Math was my strong suit. I shouldn't be worried. Yet, a lot of things I thought weren't my thing had been distracting me lately. Break the cycle. I had to break the cycle, now or never.

Just as I entered the classroom, my phone vibrated. There was a bit of hesitation to check, not knowing what to expect, hoping whatever I read wouldn't remain a lingering thought as I completed my exam. I glanced, promising myself I wouldn't respond, just take a look.

Oh so now you remember my existence

I rolled my eyes, not knowing what else I expected and turned my phone to silent, the professor walking the rows of desks and laying the exam on them. I took a deep breath as the paper landed in front of me.

"Let's do this," I whispered.

As I looked at the first problem, I could breathe a sigh of relief. I just needed to focus, and this would be a breeze.

After turning in my exam to the professor, the first thing my brain thought to do was check my phone. Respecting class rules, I pulled it out once I walked out, noticing another four missed messages from Jordyn. Rather than respond at this point, I checked the time and tried calling her. Not a second after clicking call, her voice came through.

"Seriously? What is wrong with you? You get lost for two whole frickin days?"

"Jordyn, please. Yeah, I'm doing fine, thanks. Well, that's the lie I would have told you if you kept going on. Really, we need to talk."

"Like, no duh. I've been trying but you keep ignoring my texts."

"I just got out of an exam. Where are you at? I'll head to you."

"I'm at the food court."

"Are you gonna be there long? You've got class in what, like twenty minutes?"

"I'm probably not going today. Just a lecture, nothing special."

I shook my head, always in disbelief of the ones who just willingly miss class without a reason. Financial insecurity must not be carved into their memories like it was with mine.

"I'm heading that way now."

"Copy that."

She hung up.

As I walked to the food court, I could feel eyes following me. Paranoia struck and I turned every which way, not knowing which direction it came from. My eyes land on a couple of guys kicking a soccer ball between them as they chatted. He was with them.

I turned away and didn't even consider looking back. I had no time for this.

When I arrived at the food court, Jordyn had two empty, cardboard boxes of food takeout in front of her. She always liked two breakfast sandwiches to start off the day and always went with American cheese, because for some reason no other went so well with fried egg. I wasn't going to judge her food habits, as my breakfast was no more than a prepackaged cinnamon roll. However, the smells of the food court caused my stomach to rumble, food the best distraction from the hole I felt I was digging.

"So, you finally remembered you had a friend, eh?" Jordyn crossed her arms and squinted at me, irritation evident in her tone.

"Listen, a lot has happened. Not that that's any excuse. You still have every right to hate me."

"Okay, I don't hate you." She folded the lids of the takeout containers down and threw them in a bag on the floor. "I just, I'm getting nervous about this poetry night thing, and I really want your opinion on some things."

"Well then, give it to me. Show me what you got."

"Actually, you tell me first. I'm curious what you were doing when you said you were busy."

I took a seat and sighed. Her eyes grew, realizing it was time to hear some drama. I told her everything from going to his practice, to him inviting me out, to Sara's breakdown yesterday. Her jaw continuously dropped an additional inch with every juicy detail I revealed.

"But wait, she doesn't know you two went on a date?"

I shrugged.

"I don't think so."

"You think he knew before he invited you? Like revenge?"

A pit filled my throat and I felt dizzy.

"I, uh, I definitely considered that."

"What a douche!"

I giggled, her reaction enough to make me feel better about the situation. She pulled out a bottle of orange juice and handed it to me.

"I can't."

"I already finished mine, got one with each sandwich. Some special or other."

I accepted and set it on the table, sliding it from one hand to the other.

"Well, are you gonna let me see what you've got so far. Or are you distracting me cause you're too nervous to actually show me?"

"I mean, it's just some stupid thing anyway. I might not even do this."

"What are you on about? Of course you're doing this. You have to. You're too talented not to."

Jordyn rested her head on her hand and sighed. A slight grin crossed for a split second, eyes wandering the area past me not knowing how to respond.

"I don't know it's just... it's just dumb really."

"Hear me out, it's not dumb. You're not dumb. If you love something, you gotta chase after it. No one's gonna do it for you."

Jordyn scratched at the side of her head, scrunching her lips and nose.

"Okay, fine."

She dug into her backpack and pulled out a notebook. I smiled as she flipped past several pages of class notes, defying any expectation I had of her. Notes slowly transformed to pages of doodles which changed into blocks of text, possibly related to one another, possibly not. She stopped at a page that looked more like a riddle than a poem. Squiggly lines and arrows pointed from one sentence to another halfway down the page. Words were scribbled in the margins in any way she could find to squeeze it in.

"Okay. You are going to have to read this to me. I suck at puzzles."

Jordyn laughed and tucked her swooping bangs behind her ear.

"So, it's called Breaking From the Mirror and it's about finding yourself through friendships."

Jordyn read through the best she could, also getting confused by her maze of arrows. After every line, she would stop to explain the meaning. I listened intently, nodding and smiling. Guilt filled me as I listened, having ignored her messages for two days to pursue Chase, abandoning the only friendship I needed.

But I hadn't really been after just another friendship. I wanted more than that, even though I understood what that would mean. How could a relationship built on one cheating ever include the promise of loyalty?

Jordyn finished reading her poem, biting her lip as she glanced at my expression from over her sheet of paper. I stood and gave her a standing ovation. Several of the students and employees in the food court peered in my direction, squinting eyes confused about what was happening. Jordyn covered her face with her notebook.

"And you seriously questioned whether you should do poetry night? You shouldn't just do that. You should submit this to the university's journal."

Jordyn blushed and set her notebook on the table, glancing at the text. She inhaled deeply and a huge smile sprung to her face.

"Thanks, Alex. You're a great friend."

I returned to my seat with a smile, raising again slightly as I felt my phone vibrate in my back pocket. What was once genuine happiness became forced as I read the message to come through.

Do you have time to talk?

To the side of the message was the profile picture used by Chase.

Chapter Nine

World civilizations dragged on, Jordyn scribbling more words in the back of her notebook as I stared out the window to the leaves swaying in the trees. As the winds picked up, it took with it more leaves, stripping the trees of what it spent all summer making just for it to have to start over come spring.

I had turned my phone on silent, hoping no more distractions would make it through for the day. I debated how to respond to his message. A pit fell in my stomach, an odd mixture of nerves and anger yet desire making me nauseous. Denying that I wanted to see him again proved worthless. But I could never excuse doing so.

Maybe I just had to do it, say what needed to be said, and move on. Tell him how I felt, how he used me, how he twisted my feelings to make himself feel better. I just needed to tell him to leave me alone. That was the best way, the only way, to move on from all of this.

The professor dismissed us, Jordyn reaching for my notebook as we packed up so she could copy my notes. I rolled my eyes and met hers with a smile.

"You want to see if there are any pods open? I'll copy your notes and we can pull up a movie or something."

"Actually, I have something I need to get done," I responded, that horrid feeling of guilt returning. "Maybe tonight, I'll have to see how things go. Hopefully it won't take long."

A skeptical glare crossed her face as she tried to read through my cryptic response. With a scrunched nose and mouth, she stared at me for a moment before she relaxed and shrugged.

"Suit yourself, just let me know. See ya."

As we split ways, I pulled out my phone. He hadn't followed up, not with another request, invite, a message apologizing for sending it to the wrong person. Nothing. I took a deep breath and typed.

Where do you want to meet?

Without more than a second passing, I noticed the icon change, that he had read the message. A bubble appeared to show he responded.

How about Hinton's Park?

A tremble coursed through me. This park was at the edge of campus, farm fields to one side, and forest on two others. There were several trails and picnic arrangements. It was large, plenty of space for privacy, and probably to hide a body. As the thought passed, I gulped.

Okay

I put on my coat and knit headband before walking to the park. My fingers fidgeted in my pockets for the whole walk. The incoming thoughts were like a barrage, distraction too great to pay attention to any audio book. I started repeating calculus formulas as somehow it had become my go-to in calming my heart rate.

When I arrived, I sat at a table and observed the others who decided this cold day was a great opportunity to get out. Many middle-aged people jogged with their dogs, some college students walked the trails, headphones in, taking a break from the stress of tests and decisions that would affect the rest of their life.

My legs bounced up and down, my eyes checking the environment around me, my phone, and then back to my surroundings. I probably looked super suspicious, like I was there for some sort of drug deal with the way I fidgeted and failed to sit calmly.

He came into view, the deep purple hoodie he wore made my heart accelerate, as the color made his brown eyes pop. The moment our eyes connected, a smile formed on his face. It took everything in me not to do the same.

"Thanks for meeting me here," he said when he drew near. He took a seat next to me.

"No, it's fine."

I bit my lip and looked to the ground. Everything I wanted to say, all those lines I had rehearsed as I walked to the park, were gone. My mind went blank. I wanted no more than to tell him off with all those quips and satisfying phrases, but I couldn't think of any of them.

"I just, I think I need to clear up some things. You know, concerning this past week."

"Yeah, I think you do."

He frowned and glanced up to the sky, his fingers gripping at the edge of the wooden picnic bench we sat on. My foot tapped double speed on the concrete slab, nerves and cold more so than irritation, though I think he read it differently.

"Do you want to walk and talk?"

He stood and offered me a hand to stand. The audacity.

"Sure."

I accepted his invitation without falling for the bait of his helping hand. It was him testing the waters, seeing where I was on matters. No doubt I came off as a bit hostile, but I couldn't lower my guard. Not after everything I had been through. Despite my physical attraction to him never wavering, I couldn't help but fight the urge to have any sort of emotional attraction. That's when heart break happens. That's when grief takes over, and depression and loneliness. I couldn't give in.

We walked to a trail and followed it into the forest. Silence fell between us. My mind still drew a blank as to all I wished to tell him. He hesitated to speak, not sure where to begin. After several minutes passed, he spoke.

"Getting really cold out now, isn't it?"

I turned to him, not amused. He licked his lips as he chuckled at the ground.

"I'm pathetic, aren't I?"

"Just a little," my words mumbled, despite wanting to scream it.

"Listen, I just wanted to talk to you about what happened the other day. Things didn't happen how I think you think they may have."

I furrowed my brow, a defensive stubbornness revealing itself.

"You think I read into it wrong? Which part? The one where you invited me out as just friends knowing how it would seem if anyone else found out? Or the part where you knew Sara was cheating on you, so you used me to get your revenge?"

"None of that is true. And I had every reason to be mad at Sara, but I wouldn't steep to evening the playing field."

"So, asking me, her roommate, out to eat was just a spur of the moment kind of thing?" My voice continued to display my anger. I doubted his intentions, I doubted his reasons for wanting to talk with me to clear the air. What was he trying to gain? It felt like it was a sick game to him, toying with mine and Sara's emotions.

"What was so bad about it?"

"We almost never talked before. You just decide to invite me out a couple days after finding out she's seeing someone else, like there's no correlation at all?"

"Why do those things have to connect?"

I stopped in the path, only after ensuring no one else was nearby at this part of the trail, and stared at him in shock.

"You really don't get it. You used me to get back at her. Do you feel vindicated? Do you?"

Chase paused; his jaw opened as if to speak but no words came out. He blinked in quick succession, clearly understanding something that I couldn't see.

A jogger with a dog came into view. I turned around and continued walking. It took him a moment to realize, needing to sprint to catch up.

"So, just one question. What does revenge look like to you?"

His voice was calm, oddly soothing and melodic. I hated that he still had the ability to make my heart race and my stomach flutter with nerves of being near him.

"It looks like what you did. Doing the same thing someone else did to hurt your feelings to prove how much it hurts. To make them hurt like you did." I felt tears forming in my eyes. I couldn't even look at him. I wanted to collapse into his arms, feel his embrace to comfort me from the very pain he inflicted on me. To warm up to his muscles wrapping about me with the slight pressure of healing. For so long I wished to press my lips against his again, the one-week anniversary of doing so quickly approaching. My legs trembled, my breathing grew shallow, but I kept walking, staring at the ground and putting one foot in front of the other.

A hand fell on my shoulder, pulling me from my swirling thoughts. A gentle weight, placed there temporarily to grab my attention, but how I wanted it to stay. With a slight pressure to his outer fingers, he silently asked me to turn towards him. His other hand caught under my chin, tilting my head up to meet his eyes. The warm caress of his fingers woke the butterflies in my stomach with full force.

"If it was revenge, I would have made certain that she knew, that someone else would have made sure that she knew, about us grabbing a bite to eat. I didn't tell anyone."

I opened my mouth to speak but only shallow breaths left. I had no way to refute his claim, as I believed him. If Sara knew about what happened, I surely would have heard about it not a second after. She would curse me and threaten me, she would go to many lengths, sacrificing her entire education just to get back. But her biggest concern was that she was figured out, that Chase knew about her relationship on the side.

Chase understood I had no reason to doubt his words. The hand under my chin moved to cup my cheek. The cold day stood no chance at getting a shiver out of me now. My entire body heated, my heart racing as if I'd run a marathon.

"But..." I whispered, trying to get my strength back, trying to win this argument I supposedly wanted us to have. I tried to convince myself of all he had done wrong, of all the reasons I needed to tell him off, send him away, ensure he never spoke to me again. And yet, with his slight touch, I was thankful I hadn't remembered any of the lines I wanted to use to put him on blast. I bit my tongue, not wanting my thoughts to escape me as nerves coursed through.

A smile crossed his face as silence fell between us again. He grabbed my hand, threading his fingers through mine, and led me to the bridge crossing a creek. Gentle sounds of water running under us, crunching leaves as squirrels ran about collecting more for their food stores, met our ears. We sat at a bench on the bridge, breathing in the environment around us.

"Look over there!"

He pointed in excitement as deer crossed through the shallow creek up ahead. A joyous glitter sprung to his eyes, contagious, forcing a smile from me. Two deer, one looking in our direction before trotting away.

His hand remained in mine, never letting go after we sat. I felt his warmth, slightly sweaty palms pressing against mine, wondering if he could feel my speeding pulse. What had once been anger transformed into confusion as I began to consider that which transpired.

"But..." I mumbled again, getting his attention, his smile dropping from him. "What about wanting to make up with Sara? You two fought and then you wanted to work things out. You came over. You two did, whatever you did, and apparently everything is all fine again. What about that? You can't just..." I pulled my hand from his, puzzle pieces connecting that shouldn't.

He closed his eyes and bit his lip, putting his hands into his hoodie pocket.

"Look, I said some pretty awful things to Sara. Things that even though she cheated I probably shouldn't have said. I don't intend on staying with her, she knows that, I made it very clear," Chase said, his eyes found mine and all he spoke seemed genuine. But I also couldn't be sure if he was just a great liar. "It is hard to just jump out of a relationship you spent so much time trying to make work. If she refuses to change, I don't have any other choice."

I straightened my posture and glared.

"So, you admit that you still love her. That you do want to make it work if she can prove she cares. Am I hearing this right?"

"I already know she's not gonna change-"

"But if she does? Let's say she has some sort of 'coming to Jesus' moment, would that be enough to convince you to stay?"

His face went blank, unsure of the hole he was digging, having thought that every word he spoke would be enough to win me over, to convince me that he only had good intentions. Lines that may have worked with Sara, who wanted to be told only that which she wanted to hear, but something that would not work on me.

"Alex..."

"I'm serious you know," I cut him off, my voice trembling as I spoke. "If you're playing with my emotions, I don't appreciate it. Taking me out, covering me with your jacket, holding my hand, kissing me when you had every excuse not to, I just don't want to accept that you never felt anything."

I stood and walked to the handrail, overlooking the creek below. The water was clear and flowed downstream, passing smooth pebbles and taking detours about branches and boulders in its way. I heard his footsteps draw near but refused to acknowledge it. That pressure landed on my shoulder once more, the heat permeating every layer I wore.

"What?" I voiced in frustration, annoyed, angry, just wanting to leave and curl up under my bed with a good book and some marshmallows.

I turned into his arms and was met with his lips. Smooth and sweet, a lingering taste of cherry not too far gone from his mouth. My thoughts dissolved alongside my emotions. My heart fought to escape, but only to be closer to his. And his hand assisted in its wish as he placed it on my lower back and pulled me closer.

My bottom lip slid into his mouth. Moist and rich was the taste of his upper lip as I pulled it in. His other hand found my head, holding me there not out of force, but to demonstrate his desire to never let go, to never stop.

My thoughts spiraled and tears formed in my eyes, streaming down my cheeks. The first to fall on his finger caused him to pause and pull away. Chase bit his lip, a frown growing on his face. He stepped away.

I couldn't stop the tears from flowing. I couldn't stop my breathing from becoming erratic.

"I'm sorry. I didn't realize..."

"I'm so confused."

I leaned against the rail to support me, my knees trembling as I started to feel faint and dizzy. A rush of hormones and emotions caused my blood pressure to jump then plummet. The pit in my stomach expanded, causing cramps and nausea.

My eyes connected with his and I noticed a tear forming in the corner of his eye. I buried my head into my hands and sobbed, my shoulders rising and falling uncontrollably. A quaking hand found my back and pulled me into an embrace.

I hated every moment. Being in a public place, crying and looking pathetic. My ears perked at every sound, paranoid someone passing by would take notice. I flinched at every sensation to cross my body, from my own strands of hair poking at my face or tickling my neck as the breeze passed.

"No one's coming," he said, as if able to hear my thoughts. "Just let it out."

He tried to give me a safe space, a place in his arms where I felt like I could belong. But that space in those arms, it wasn't for me. It was reserved for Sara. No, he wasn't property, he could allow anyone into that space that he wanted, but it didn't feel right. As long as he could voice his love for another, that space wasn't for me. Though invited, I didn't feel welcome.

I came to and reversed out of his arms. My arms wiped across my face, tears and mucus smearing across the sleeves of my jacket. I couldn't bring myself to care.

"I have to go," I mumbled, not only telling him but trying to convince myself that it was the only thing I could do at that point. My fists clenched and, with a deep breath, I headed back to the path out of the forest.

"Please, just know I'm sorry for all of this. I hope you can forgive me," he said as I took a few steps.

I paused for a moment, wondering if I should respond, but no response was necessary. The cold finally hit with a gust of wind that found every path through my clothing to call a chill up my spine. A crunch of leaves occurred behind me as I listened to every one of his steps. He kept his distance, continuing behind me until out of the park.

Chapter Ten

A few days passed and I heard nothing more from Chase. I spent as much time with Jordyn that weekend as I possibly could, even joining her for band night at The Lounge. We rocked to music and discussed her poetry, the live reading only a week away.

"I was actually thinking," Jordyn yelled at me over the music blaring in our faces given our seats in front of a speaker. "If I get enough of these poems written, I could like sell them as a book."

"That would be awesome!"

I sipped at a sour watermelon, strawberry iced drink, wondering if I would ever go back to my classic pick. It wasn't a bad substitute, and it came with a lot less memory and baggage than the other one. Granted, the best part was Jordyn's priceless reaction when I placed my order, as if the world was ending.

"I just can't believe that in a week, one of my dreams will come true."

"You might have to change your major to creative writing at this point."

"I definitely have considered it. Just, ugh, change scares me."

I shook my head and laughed at her response. If there was ever anyone who seemed absolutely fearless to that which would cause my anxiety to spiral it would be Jordyn.

"So, what's up with you?" Jordyn asked, raising a leg up on her chair and pulling it to her chest.

"What do you mean?"

"You've been super-duper serious and like, almost like, sad, lately. I don't know, check some T-O-X-I-C toxic energy, you know."

"Sorry for being so toxic, I guess."

"Bitch, you know what I mean. You are not you. And you know why. But *you*," Jordyn placed extra emphasis on the word, pointing at me with a twirling finger, "refuse to tell me for some reason."

"A lot has happened this past week. It's all somewhat a bit overwhelming really."

"This has to do with Chase, right? Chase the douche? Chase the asshole? What did he do now, or is he just living rent free in your head?"

I licked my lips and suppressed a chuckle at her response, while understanding full well that she wanted me to talk about it. I hated feeding into any sort of drama. I loathed the thought that Jordyn may slip up and say something to the wrong person. Not that she would mean to, she just couldn't control herself sometimes. Deciding to take the plunge, to trust in my best friend and get this pressure off my chest, I recounted what happened at the park.

As my story went on, her jaw dropped more and more. When I reached the part where we kissed, her eyes grew wide. I knew full well had she been sipping at her smoothie, it would be all over the floor by now. Her bodily reactions were seemingly outside of her control as well, as arm swinging and leg kicking occurred throughout my entire tale.

"He's not the only asshole," Jordyn said, pouting her lip. "You are, too."

"Yeah, yeah, I probably am."

"There's no probably about it. You even know you shouldn't and you just can't help yourself."

"You're right."

I nodded and glanced at the floor. I felt awful already, her words stinging deeper than any thought and name I could call myself. My fingers clasped behind my head, and I tensed my arms, trying to distract myself from the tears that wanted to form.

"But that's okay. Not all assholes are bad people. Sometimes they just make a mistake. Sometimes they're just shitty, but not all the time."

"How do I come back from this?" I leaned on the table, discussing the topic enough to exhaust me. "I'm supposed to be here to study, to take my classes and get a job that makes it so that I never have to go back home. Why are there so many distractions in a place meant to foster excellence?"

"No one ever accused universities of being distraction free. And they also aren't credited as institutions that only have people achieving excellence, quite the opposite actually."

"Jordyn, I've never been in this kind of situation before. How do you just forget about someone? In the past, my relationships have always been trainwrecks, leaving those boys behind an obvious choice. But this is so different. We haven't even gotten the chance to know each other."

"If he does like you, don't you think he would have left Sara by now? Just a thought."

"I don't know. I get that he's kind of sensitive, you know, like he doesn't want to hurt her feelings."

"Ugh," Jordyn sticks out her tongue and fakes a gag.

"What?" A grin crosses my face. "It's sweet." Jordyn raises an eyebrow. "It just kind of sucks that he's in a relationship he can't figure out how to leave. If he really even wants to."

"I swear, y'all are living in a soap opera. I gotta use some of this for my next poem. It will be titled 'To Love and to Maybe Be Loved, Just Not Sure Yet, and am Unprepared for Emotional Devastation.'"

We both laughed and went to the bar to order some food. When we returned to the table, she pulled out her notebook and we discussed her works in process. The visuals and feelings she brought to life through words were truly spectacular. To find one's passion must be a feeling that compared to none other. Perhaps it was even similar to finding true love. I doubted I would ever know the feeling of either.

After a long evening, I returned to my room, ready to rest up for an early day of studying and homework starting the next day. I had brought a bottle of lemonade, licking my lips as the taste lingered there. My phone hovered over my face, getting in my social media binging before bed. The moment I saw his face enter my feed, I turned off the screen immediately, refusing to give in to any temptation whatsoever.

I stared at the ceiling and daydreamed about what the perfect relationship would be to me. Trying to replace any thought of him with the image of a famous actor.

"I would want someone who respected my emotions, who believes in consent and equality. Someone who can empathize and show compassion. Sensitive."

Why did I say that word? His face immediately sprung to mind. I rubbed at my eyes, trying to unsee it. The more I connected to a memory of him, the more doomed I would be. He already ruined orange tasting anything, I didn't want to give up an actual, working vocabulary because too much would link back to him.

My phone vibrated, causing me to jump. I thanked God for the distraction at least. I turned on the screen and rolled my eyes. It was my mom.

Tom and I are passing by on a casino tour our travel agent put together. Would be great to grab some lunch. Let me know what you're thinking.

The fact she even used the words 'travel agent' and 'casino' made me shake my head, knowing in their financial situation they should not be traveling or gambling, doing both just absolute peril to anything remaining in their bank accounts. The thought of having to suffer through a lunch with both of them made me wonder if I'd even be able to stomach the food.

Probably just with me. It would be on Friday

I sighed in relief, but only that her boyfriend wouldn't be there. Despite my desire to do anything but attempting to bond with her, I just wanted a motherly figure there for me for this one moment of my life. I never believed she could give good relationship advice, her own love life an absolute disaster. But maybe I could pick up snippets of wisdom from her own experiences. Maybe I just hoped to hear the words I wished someone would tell me. And if there was ever a person to feed into my delusion, it would be her.

As I went to respond, I heard a slam against the door, making me jump. Jingling keys and panicked voices sounded, no words distinct enough to make out, though the distressed tone of Sara was obvious.

The door swung open, Sara was bawling with Bridgette and Cassidy following close behind. I sat up in my bed and stared at the group, trying to figure out what happened. Cassidy rushed to make Sara's favorite drink in the instant cup coffee maker and Bridgette patted Sara's shoulder and offered her a box of tissues.

"Is everything okay?" I questioned, not wanting to be out of the loop.

"No," was the only word Sara could mumble before she started sobbing again. She forced a pillow to her face and screamed into it in her grief. Bridgette clenched her jaw as she leaned away, as if afraid her friend was rabid.

Cassidy stepped away from the machine while it ran and, stopping at the edge of my bed, covered one side of her mouth and directed her words at me.

"Chase just broke up with her."

My jaw dropped. My heart pounded, feeling sympathy for Sara yet something else existed there. I felt so many emotions at one time I thought I would puke. My desire to leave, to run from the room and find Jordyn grew, but I was paralyzed. My mind burst with conflicting thoughts, wondering, just wondering what would happen next.

Chapter Eleven

Sunday, my day for studying and homework, became a day of gossip and scouting information. I sat on the rug in Jordyn's dorm room, eating a bowl of instant noodles. My textbook was open on one side, a notebook on the other, neither having had a page flipped in over an hour.

I swiped through my phone, searching to see that it was all true. Jordyn and I verified that both of their relationship statuses changed, though Sara's was set to 'It's complicated,' Jordyn rolling on the floor in laughter. I checked Chase's online status. It said he was there, it said he was online. I refreshed my messages over and over again. Nothing.

"Maybe he's just not ready to jump into another relationship. You know? Because he's sensitive."

I flipped her off.

"Shut up with that. Guys are allowed to have feelings, too."

She shook her head as she mocked my words and jumped into her bed.

"You think all those emo songs the bands you listen to sing are because they're hard-hearted? They just choose to process their emotions differently."

"Yeah, yeah. I know you're right, but I still think he's a douche. Though, maybe a bit less of one now."

"And you are free to hold that opinion."

I put my phone down and actually went over some definitions for a biology exam later in the week. My calculus book stared at me, reminding me of the equations I could be memorizing to distract myself.

"Have you finalized your poem?"

Jordyn moaned and kicked her legs into the air.

"I thought I had. But then I reread it and realized it sucks. I probably just have to start over at this point, which fuckin' sucks."

I reached over and nudged her arm, ensuring she could see my expression.

"You absolutely are not starting over. Now you're just too much in your head. Relax and look at it again when you have a clearer headspace."

"Maybe you're right." Jordyn slid from her bed to sit next to me. "Hey, why don't you write a poem, since you're so stuck in your feelings right now."

I rolled my eyes and shrugged off her question.

"Seriously, it can be such a release."

"Yea, not really my thing."

My fingers flipped through the pages of my textbook, still unable to take in information, but no longer wishing to talk.

As I headed back to my room, I scrolled through my phone, refreshing every minute to see if her status had changed. If anyone were post their life's play by play on their social media, Sara took the prize. I hated myself and the obsession I allowed to overcome me.

"Why can't I be like Jordyn? Why can't I find something else to love, to strive after, a passion I can chase that isn't just him? Am I seriously so-"

My phone vibrated and caused me to jump. It was his picture.

"Damn it," I mumbled, thinking my intentions would manifest if I focused hard enough. He was the last distraction I needed right now.

Can we talk?

I bit my lip and paused, not wanting to walk through the door to the room and see Sara's face. I tapped my toe, thinking through all the possible ways I could respond. I stopped and listened. My heart, it didn't accelerate as it once had when I saw his name. Perhaps I had broken the spell...

But I needed closure, or else he would never be gone from my mind. This felt a bit déjà vu.

Not today

I didn't want to ignore him, but hopefully my response would get him thinking. I saw the bubble appear that meant he was typing. I waited, checking all areas around to ensure no one saw. The last thing I needed was for Sara to find out now.

The bubble with ellipses bounced in place. After a minute it disappeared, no message sent. I sighed.

I entered the dorm room and threw my phone on my bed, not wanting anymore temptations, not wanting anymore distractions. I opened my books and began my studying, as I should have done hours ago.

The next day, as I endured class as always, I doodled away in my notebook. I debated whether I even needed to study, the lessons slowing and growing repetitive. As I peeked about the room, I noticed many others barely paying attention to the droning of the professor, and I doubted they cared to study on their weekends.

Entire pages of my notebook were now dedicated to my drawings. What started as squiggly lines, turned into elaborate vines. Flowers that were once alone now stood alongside a garden. I even ensured the leaves were of the proper shape, utilizing my phone to maximize accuracy. They were no longer just doodles but intricate art.

Oddly enough, I sighed in anguish when the professor dismissed us, hoping to continue growing my garden. I had some time before my next class, and with nothing else to do, I headed to the bleachers outside to add to my imaginary safe space from reality.

The weather was cool but sitting in the sun provided just the right amount of warmth that I wouldn't have to completely bundle up. Perfect for a hoodie and my leather boots and leg warmers. The field before the stands was empty but for a student or two passing a frisbee to one another. Most other students walked, biked, or jogged to their next classes. I sat there as no more than an observer.

With a deep breath in, my fingers twirling my pencil in my hand, I put graphite to paper and started drawing that which blossomed in my mind on the page.

Trees rose from mossy rocks, dew drop particles formed on unopened blossoms, as a jungle came to life amidst the white paper with blue lines. I used my pencil to crosshatch on some rocks and boulders. Then I practiced shading with a tree's canopy and the shadow within.

My mind relaxed, transporting me to a time years back. In junior high, my art had made it into the school art show. I beamed with pride as I presented the note of acceptance to my mom. My stepdad had scoffed, saying art shows at schools were like no more than participation trophies, anyone could get in. I held back tears as I showed my mom the invitation to the showing, an open house for parents and the students. I remembered her eyeing the date. She looked to my stepdad then back at me. With a sigh, she handed the invitation back to me and shook her head. Her husband had a softball game that night, a team from his company against other out-of-shape, middle-aged men.

"Maybe next time," she said.

"You should invest your time in something that will land you a job, you know, actually make money," he smirked and grabbed my mom by the waist, kissing at her neck.

I left and returned to my room. There wouldn't be a next time.

A tear formed in my eye just thinking of the child, lost and alone. Passion was never propagated. Perhaps the ability to love was also abandoned in time.

In wanting to forget, anything and everything, I lost myself to the forest. Another tree, cracking through a stump, a toadstool for good luck, bromeliad and orchids blooming in the trees, grass and wildflowers mixing with grounded leaves. It was a world of wonder, a world of beauty, an escape that was mine, only for me, just for...

A soccer ball rolled up to the stands in front of my feet. I flinched and muttered a curse, my fantasy breaking as reality infringed. Granted, maybe it was better rolled up to my feet than hitting me square in the face, since I wouldn't have known what hit me. Feet entered my peripheral vision, jogging in the grass to meet the ball sent my way. My eyes moved up the frame and I almost leapt from my seat.

"Chase..."

"Alex."

A smile spread across his face as he stopped in front of me. Not even by force could I twist my mouth to a grin, a frown the best I could muster.

"I meant to text you back, I did. I just thought you really didn't want to talk anyway."

"Well, you weren't wrong," I replied, closing my notebook before reconnecting with his eyes. My answer forced his smile to vanish, mirroring my own expression.

"But just like I said, you seem to be everywhere."

A giggle I wasn't anticipating left me, his surprise perhaps equal to mine. His hand reached to jostle the hair behind his head.

"So, what have you been up to?" Chase asked, his attempt to initiate conversation enough to force me to relax a bit.

"Studying, homework, you know, the typical day of a student in their freshman year."

His expression softened, understanding that even if I wished to never see him again, responding to his question with an actual answer was more than enough of a sign to keep pushing. My fingers fidgeted, playing with the metal spiral of my notebook, wondering if I should keep engaging, keep giving him hope. A false hope. Was I just as bad as him now? Was I toying with his emotions just to let him down, watch him fall? I had made up my mind...

"I've been trying to do more of that stuff to. Classes are still pretty chill, but next semester I've got some difficult ones lined up. Need to start making habits, you know?"

I treated his question as rhetorical and slid my notebook into my backpack. I wished to return to the jungle on the page, continue drawing my imaginary world, one where I didn't have to deal with drama and boys. A world where it was just me, alone.

"Before you go." Chase waved his hands to grab my attention. My eyes met his. "Look, I'm an idiot and there's not enough ways to say I'm sorry. But I do want to make it up to you."

"We've already crossed that bridge-"

"Please." Chase licked his lips, his eyes scanning about for any further words he could use as a net. He found his soccer ball on the ground by my feet. "Okay, look. I'll goal keep and you kick."

"Chase," I said with a breathy chuckle.

"If I stop the ball, I get one more chance, just one more. But if you get it passed me, I'll never talk to you again. That's a promise."

My eyes found his, desperation and pleading. I felt awful. I had never wanted the roles to be reversed. Just as I once longed for him, felt like I needed his attention, his affection to feel complete, he now begged with me for that chance. I had lacked those things for so many months now, I would grow numb to it again once the memory passed. But he only just got out of a relationship. He had not numbed to the longing and the desire of having someone to share a hug with, someone to take care of and them take care of you in return. He had not forgotten about the need of affection to feel happy, attention to feel purposeful. His words were no more than those of a person who grieved loss of love and searched in vain for a small glimpse that it could happen again.

I stood and glanced at my bag and then at the soccer ball. With a sigh, I stepped from the bleachers, leaving my bag behind and taking to the field. A smile crossed his face.

"Fine," I responded. "But just know that I was the top in my state for two years in high school. And I'm not too far out of practice that I couldn't get a shot past you."

"Seriously?" His jaw dropped in surprise.

"No," I laughed.

"I seriously thought for a second that you were just gonna rainbow it right past me like a pro."

"I have no idea what you just said."

Chase scratched at his head as he laughed, lifting the ball with his toe into his hands. We walked to the field.

My nerves built as I knew I would never get it past him.

"It's just one more date, suck it up," I mumbled, trying to convince myself that I didn't want it. Why would I want to go out with him again, just us, acting like it was fine that it would be the last time. Acting like I was fine that we would never talk to one another again, never kiss one another again... I shivered, a pit falling into my stomach as the sensations and emotions that accompanied memories found their way to me.

Chase set the ball on the field, circling around it and eyeing the goal to ensure it was where he wanted it.

"We'll start it here," he said after moving it a couple millimeters this way and that. "Now, you don't have to kick it from here. You just have to start the play from here."

"Okay."

"Are you ready?"

"Sure."

Chase jogged to the goal and took a defensive stance.

"Give me your worst," he shouted with a laugh.

"Yeah, my..." An idea flashed before me as my competitive nature was wakened. Even if I didn't want to win given his terms, I had to.

"Just one question. What's the proper way to actually kick it?" I eyed the ball and tapped my foot against it at all angles.

"I mean, you don't want to use your toes. Unless of course you want it to grab some air. But to prevent injury, use the side of your foot and angle it towards me."

I crossed my arms and squatted by the ball.

"But, if it stays on the ground the whole way, it will lose speed to friction. Shouldn't I want it to go through the air rather than stay on the ground?"

"I mean whatever works for you."

Chase dropped his stance and observed me walking around the ball. I couldn't tell if he was irritated or just confused at how ignorant I was of the sport.

"Can you just show me real quick?"

He sighed and jogged over. As he almost came to a complete stop at my side, I kicked the ball with the side of my foot, straight through his legs and darted for the open goal. With little effort, I dipped my toe under and kicked it through the air to the corner of the net. In actuality, I was lucky I could get close enough to make it.

He yelled after me, laughing all the while.

"That's not fair. I totally thought, ugh," he growled in an amused frustration.

I laughed, trying to catch my breath as my heart raced. I hadn't run like that in months, not ever having the need to. Seeing his expression, running through the situation time and time again, it caused me to laugh harder. I fell to the ground in exhaustion of needing to breathe and being unable to stop my laughter. Chase jogged to me and sat at my side.

We sat a moment in silence. I looked to the sky and noticed the clouds growing grayer as the day went on. A chilly breeze that I hadn't even noticed had started, accompanied them. As I glanced at him, I noticed he had already been looking at me. His eyes met mine then slowly made their way to my lips. My heart raced faster than it had earlier.

With a shaky exhale, Chase stood and grabbed his soccer ball. "Looks like you won. I'll respect our deal. It was nice knowing you." He turned his back to me and trudged toward the path.

"Hey!" I yelled after him. He rotated to look at me.

"So what time are we meeting? Same place, right? And are we meeting there since you have practice first or do you want to come get me when you're ready?"

A grin refused to be a smile on his face, forcing back his excitement. My own happiness exploded, the pit disappeared, as I understood the feelings were reciprocated. Even if it was just him needing to get over the breakup, I could be there for him. I would be there for him. And hopefully, when I needed it most, he would be there for me.

Chapter Twelve

The next couple of days couldn't move fast enough. Every moment I thought about what I would wear, what we would say, how I would keep hiding it from Sara. Whenever I would text him and she was in the room, my peripheral vision was acutely aware of her every position. Even a glance in my direction would cause me to turn to ensure she would never be able to see a word of our conversations. Not that I should care anymore. They were no longer together. And Sara had already moved on as well.

"You think it's alright? I mean it's only been a couple of days. You don't think people will start talking?" Sara spoke to assumedly Bridgette on the other end. It was always about some gossip, some drama, he said she said. "But before we just laughed it off. But now... Now people will say things." A pause. "As if, everyone knows she's just a basic bitch." Sara cackled. "Totes, totes. You're right. I can't let it ruin my night. You're the best. See you soon." Sara smooched at the phone speaker before hanging up.

She let out a long, exaggerated sigh and I felt her eyes on me. I turned off my phone screen before giving her any of my attention.

"Don't ever get into a relationship, m'kay. They're just messy."

"Thanks for the advice," I voiced sarcastically, not understanding why she felt the need to tell me. It's not like she knew I was seeing anyone, especially him. If she knew, she would have kicked me out of our room by now.

Sara grabbed her purse and rushed out the door, her yelling at Bridgette as she came into view loud and clear through the solid, and shut, door. I took a deep breath and grabbed my pencil and notebook. My garden expanded every day. Petals with a heart like shape sprinkled the path to a beautiful fountain. The area all about it was grey and littered with eraser shavings. I couldn't get the water to look real, every attempt as ugly and frustrating as the first.

My phone buzzed and before I saw the message, I looked at the time. With a startled jump, I went to my closet and dug out the nicest dress and matching leggings I could find. Remembering the alert to pull me to attention, I read the message bubble that arrived next to his name.

Ready when you are. Just waiting in the courtyard below.

His message was followed by a smiley face. My heart and stomach fluttered. I got dressed, lightly spritzed some perfume, and giggled as I absolutely ignored my roommate's advice. Maybe relationships were messy, but if there's never anything to clean than how can strong bonds ever be formed?

I raced down the stairs, with utmost care as being agile and graceful at the same time was definitely not my strong suit. When I see him in the courtyard, I slow my movements and try to collect my breathing.

"Wow, Alex, you look great."

His smile grows as I approach, gentle eyes scanning me from head to toe. The breeze sends a whiff of his cologne to me, the smell intoxicating and forcing raised bumps up my arm. Luckily, I remembered to put on his sweatshirt that had been hiding under my bed before I left.

"You recognize this?" I laughed, pulling at the hoodie strings and sticking out my tongue.

Chase bit his bottom lip and nodded, the memory of him leaving it to me not a pleasant one apparently. With a sigh, he extended a hand.

"We should get going. It's gonna start getting colder, and I can't think of many ways to keep you warm out here."

My face grew hot as nerves swept through me; a hormonal rush hit. My hand fell into his and we walked a path the two of us had walked several times before. And as with everything before, this memory would carve itself into me, so that every time after, when I walked that path, I would remember the first time his warmth radiated through me. A warmth that for the first time was all mine.

We arrived at the diner, the salty, savory smells and rush of heat hitting as he opened the door before me. Not many were dining on this night, almost causing me greater anxiety. Blending into a crowd was easy the larger the crowd. Less people almost created a sense of less privacy, as if every word would echo from the walls. As if no secret would remain to the two of them.

He didn't appear to have the same thoughts, not bothering to hush his words as we sat.

"I actually couldn't believe it, when you said that. I don't know how I could describe to you how happy it made me to know that I could have one more chance."

"Who says it's just one?"

I bit my lip and grinned, seemingly at the tablecloth. I wanted to curse my flirtatiousness but was also impressed I was able to come up with something so clever so quickly.

"Well, that's what I hoped to convince you of," Chase smiled and nodded to the waitress as she delivered our drinks. "Seems you've made my job a lot easier now."

We ordered our meals, actual meals and not just slices of pizza this time. He replayed his embarrassment of the trick I pulled on the field, the memory causing him absolute amusement. I laughed along with him, thinking that one of my actions could cause someone so much pleasure filling me with warmth.

"So, what were you doing there anyway? Like really?"

His eyes met mine, as if daring me to say I had been waiting for him to see me. The honest truth would disappoint him.

"You know, just drawing."

"You're an artist?"

That word made me blush, as if giving me credit where it was definitely not due. I bit my lip and tilted my head back and forth, almost ashamed for my lack of skill at my age.

"I wouldn't say artist. Maybe more like an amateur doodler."

Chase swiped his hair from his eyes and took a sip of his drink, orange soda.

"Well, I would love for you to show me your work sometime. I think it's amazing what some people are able to create. It takes a lot to make something from nothing."

"That's a nice way of thinking about it. I guess I always just thought of it as a guilty pleasure, hiding it to not embarrass myself. I even stopped for a short time because my mom's husband said it was a useless skill."

"Well, fuck him. Excuse my language, but that's so stupid he could even say something like that."

My heart exploded in some surreal mix of emotions. Validation, his validation, felt so strong and comforting. I had to prevent myself from bawling. It was a strange realization of something being cured that I never knew needed healed. A part of me I never knew I had lost.

"Anyways," he continued, stirring the straw in his drink as if nerves were rising within him. "I do have a question for you."

"Okay, what's up?"

"So, there's this party coming up, and I wanted to know if you wanted to go with me?"

A sudden suck of the saliva build up in my mouth sent me into a choking fit. He panicked and slightly rose from his seat, reaching a hand across to me. I swatted it away and faked a smile, gesturing that everything was fine. I rushed to drink my soda, not realizing that adding more stuff to choke on was not going to help the situation. Tears filled my eyes, and any suppressed coughs were in vain. After about a minute of fighting it, I caught my breath and wiped my eyes, catching his expression in my embarrassment.

"I didn't realize you would absolutely hate the idea of going to a party with me," he joked and leaned back in his chair, pulling the attention from my inability to function like an actual human.

"It's not that," I giggled. "I just didn't expect that. Obviously, you have friends that will be there. People that may even know who I am. Are you sure you wanted to ask me, or you just feel obligated?"

"If you still think this is some revenge thing or a prank, it's not. There is no one pressuring me to ask you except for my own feelings hoping that you say yes."

The waitress placed our plates in front of us, the smells causing my stomach to rumble and distracting from the cramp arising in my side. My eyes avoided his as my thoughts raced. I didn't even want to think about the drama and possible fight to be caused should Sara show up. She hung out in the same social circles as Chase, even doing her best to avoid him no doubt they saw each other every now and again.

"So, is that a no?"

I hadn't realized how long I'd been lost to my thoughts. Looking him in the eyes, grin growing, I answered.

"I'd love to go. With you. I will go with you. Yes."

My stammering never failed to give away my emotions. However, a bullying joke didn't follow. His eyes lit as if the only word that mattered of it all was that I said yes.

"When is it?"

"This Saturday."

My heart sank. Of all the times to actually have something planned, why did it have to be that day?

"Oh, that's not good."

His joyous smile sank, and his brow furrowed.

"What do you mean? Already have another date or something?"

His curt hostility hit like a brick to the side of the head. The snappy response was surely something he had used with Sara before, or would have liked to knowing the outcome that faced him. Or maybe it was just a defense mechanism for having been cheated on before, and in such close proximity to him inviting me out.

"No, no. It's poetry night and my best friend has a slot. I promised I'd be there to support her."

My hands moved from my utensils to my lap as my thoughts consumed me once more. My heart pulled at me from both ways, but I couldn't have both. Or could I...

"The party is going on all night. We don't have to stay for the whole thing."

A light at the end of the tunnel.

"We could just sneak out when it's your friend's time to read."

"That's brilliant."

His hand raised behind his head, and he shrugged, as if never having been accused of an intelligent thought. But it was brilliant. I could make it work. Make the life I wanted work. I just had to be smart about it. Give them both their time and then voila, my life would be amazing with my best friend and, hopefully sooner rather than later, boyfriend.

"I'm not typically a party goer," I said, a new fear forming in my mind. "Is it less crazy the earlier we go? Or do we go after the reading?"

"It all depends who you hang out with," Chase responded, taking on a cool sort of smirk. "Also depends on where you're at. There are going to be quite a bit of people at this one, but we should be able to find a spot where we can just hang out."

"Can't we just hang out somewhere that isn't a mess with loud music and possibly drunken people?"

"It's a great conversation starter. Just watching people and laughing as they struggle to stand or fight with each other over the stupidest shit."

"Sounds like a great time." My sarcasm left a bit drier than intended. He sighed.

"I just want you to relax a bit. Not feel so tense. We can just sit and watch others. Just relax and be with each other. Sometimes those moments together make great memories."

I took up a fry to my mouth and chewed as I pondered me response.

"It's fine. I said yes, didn't I? That's really all I want, just more time with you."

I thought his happiest moment of the night had already passed, but I had been wrong. A jovial laugh escaped him, and he buried his face in his hands. Giddy and cheerful. I couldn't help but wonder if he ever acted as so with Sara. He always appeared so serious when they were together, or at least every interaction I paid attention to. It was so odd to see him break through some shell of those preconceived notions I had of him. Granted, that shell already had a major crack when he showed any interest in a person like me.

A person like me...

The more time I spent with him, I realized we had more similarities than I previously thought. Maybe it would all be fine. We could make this work. I was determined.

Chapter Thirteen

The day I dreaded had finally arrived. I tapped on my phone throughout class, hoping to see the message I envisioned in my dreams.

Sorry, honey. Gonna have to cancel.

Sorry, Alex. My boyfriend decided family doesn't actually mean anything.

Sorry, but I'm just not hungry enough to endure lunch with you.

Though I expected messages as so would never come across, it wouldn't bother me if they actually did. At this point in my life, I didn't think there was anything my mom could do to ruin our relationship any further. I respected her for the fact that she raised me. That didn't mean she wasn't going to a retirement home if it ever came down to me taking care of her.

Class was dismissed and I walked out the door, jumping at the sudden pressure on my shoulder. With a fright that could have caused me to knock someone out, I decided rather to catch my breath and turn to see the culprit.

Chase stood outside, waiting for me apparently. He held two smoothies, both alike in dignity, and handed one to me.

"I remembered what you got the last time. Hope you haven't changed your mind since then."

My heart never got used to how cute he was. And despite the rule of attraction stating that a person which was not yours will instantly be more attractive, I found it just the opposite. Being able to wrap my arms about him, knowing that they wouldn't be hugging any other with the same affection, caused my attraction for him to skyrocket. Pressing into the warmth of his hoodie and the security of his toned arms and abs, I didn't know how anyone would feel less attracted for being there.

"Thanks, you didn't have to do that."

"There's a lot of things I don't have to do. I do it because I want to."

He pulled me closer and kissed my head. A shiver traveled down my spine and the hairs on the back of my neck rose. My eyes met his, a glimmer of my happiness reflected in his brown irises. For the first time as an actual couple, I rose up on my tiptoes and planted my lips on his.

Though not as long as our other kisses, passing as soon as it came, it wasn't any less intimate. The taste of orange and vanilla, with a dash of cinnamon, passed to my lips before I could even get a taste of my smoothie. But, coming from him, it tasted so much sweeter.

"You have any plans for lunch?"

"Actually, I do."

His smile dropped and peered at the ground.

"Oh."

"It's nothing serious. It's actually pretty stupid. My mom is in town and wanted to have lunch with me."

"Shouldn't you be excited? From what I've seen, you haven't left campus for a weekend since you got here. Don't you miss her?"

"I miss her about as much as a used tissue. I really don't need to talk with her in person just to hear her complaining."

"I get it. I do. But maybe she needs to see you because she's missing you. You are her daughter."

"I may be her daughter, but she treats me like a stepdaughter she never wanted. Maybe I'm just not lovable."

Chase wrapped a hand about my waist and pulled me close to whisper in my ear.

"That's not true."

A smile crept through my frustration. I leaned my head on his chest.

"Thanks," I mumbled, relief entering me with every calm breath aligned with his own. I pulled away. "And thank you for the smoothie. But I really have to go and drop my stuff off before meeting with her."

"Just try to be understanding of her. She is your mom."

I shrugged and, before I could turn away, I felt the tug at my jacket to return. His lips met with mine, a sensation, a taste, I never wanted to end.

"Text me when you can," he said as we parted ways.

My heart raced, both with happiness for the moments and memories but also with anxiety following close behind. The many lies I could tell my mom to get out of it and return to his side multiplied as new ideas sprouted. But guilt ate away at me, and for every excuse to not go, there was a reason I should. And most all reasons pointed to Chase's words.

She is your mom.

I laid on my bed kicking at the air, our room always quiet during the day. Jordyn texted me lines she was changing in her poem, freaking out that she needed to cancel, that she couldn't do it. I tried every trick in the book to calm her down, talk her off the ledge. I reassured her time and time again of how amazing she was. Her texts turned to no more than emojis and then went silent. Exhausted by my own nerves, I set down my phone and closed my eyes.

After what felt like several minutes, I looked at my phone and jumped to see the number of texts that had flooded me. As I scrolled through, I noticed a bunch of missed calls as well. My eyes caught the time and I noticed almost an hour had passed. My mom sent me message after message, text and voicemail, asking where I was, if I was available. I hadn't realized I silenced my phone.

I jumped from my bed and messaged back.

I'm so sorry. Where are you?

I ran down the stairs and out the door, staring at my phone, awaiting a response.

I found us some seats at this nice bar and grill. Don't remember the name. The one with the bird in a basketball uniform.

I knew exactly where she was and raced across campus.

When I arrived, winded and exhausted, I took a few seconds to collect myself and fix my disheveled appearance, which she would surely comment on, before going inside. I wiped my eyes to get rid of any crusty residue and entered the restaurant.

I peeked my head to the seating area, trying to catch a glimpse.

"Can I help you?" the host asked. I wasn't sure if he wanted to help me to a seat or thought I needed medical attention due to my heaving.

"I'm just looking for-"

My eyes landed on her, and I couldn't help but slam a palm to my forehead. Permed curls were pulled back from her face with a rhinestone clip, bleach blonde with purple streaks. Light reflected like a sun glare from a pair of gaudy, faux diamond earrings. I couldn't yet see her clothes, but I doubted they were any less subtle.

"Found her."

With a mumble, I nodded to the host in thanks for his trying to attend me, and marched with resolve over to the woman I would normally call mom.

When she saw me drawing near, I could already feel her eyes scanning and judging every wrinkle in my clothes, every pimple scar on my face, my lack of care for my fading pink tips and split ends. It was not a welcoming walk to that table but more so a voluntary march to a loss of self-confidence for the day.

"Hi, mom," I said, my voice leaving without emotion. I failed to understand why I put myself through this torture.

"Oh, Alex!"

She rushed to stand and hug me, stiff arms constricting me like an embrace. She gestured to a chair, and I took a seat.

"I was starting to worry. You weren't answering my calls, and I almost called Tom to take me up to your dorm."

"Sorry to worry you. I fell asleep waiting for the time to pass, thought I set an alarm."

"Oh yes, exactly why I pay for your schooling, so you can sleep during the day."

My mom crosses her arms and squints at me, her eyes scanning every pore on my face.

"You sure it's not drugs?"

"Mom," I groaned, really not wanting to start the accusatory conversations.

"I met some college types in my younger days, it's always drugs. Or sometimes alcohol. What are those bags under your eyes?"

Her hand reached for my face, and I swatted it away.

"It's been a long couple of weeks. Like I said, I was tired and took a nap. Is it really so hard to believe just one word that comes out of my mouth?"

My mom stuck out a pouting lip and tapped her menu. Her mouth opened to speak but promptly closed.

"Sorry you had to wait," I gently said, hoping to cut through some of the tension. "Did you already order?"

A grin sprung to her face, and she shook her head.

"Not yet. I was thinking the Caesar salad or perhaps the chicken wrap. Tom thinks I need to cut back on red meats," she added in the last part as if to justify her order. Unfortunately, my pity would be wasted on her. "What looks good to you?"

"I'm thinking the deluxe grilled cheese."

I peered up at her from my menu. She barred her teeth as if wanting to comment but holding back. I could appreciate the attempt, but I knew it would slip in three, two...

"Doesn't that seem kind of fatty?"

"Yea, so what. Who cares?"

"Well, if you're ever going to get a boy..."

Her eyes looked at the ceiling above, as if suggesting I should reconsider. I folded my menu and set it down on the table. Our eyes met.

"I forgot to tell you. Actually, there is someone."

My mom's eyes grew wide, and she threw her menu down, having gossip to share with my sister and her boyfriend all she thirsted for.

The waitress arrived and took our orders. The entire time, my mom fidgeted with her menu, then with her fingers after handing the menu to our waitress. The wait to learn more, to dig deeper, quite literally was killing her. As the waitress walked away, she cracked.

"Who is it? What does he look like? Would I know him? Is he a nice boy?"

I held my hands up to stop her right there.

"Answer your mother. This is information I need to be made privy to, preferably right when it happens."

"Well," I started, my eyes darting from hers as the stare grew more intense by the second. "His name is Chase. He's a soccer player-"

"Ooh."

"What?"

"An athlete, huh? So, he's got to be pretty fit and lean. Probably takes super good care of himself, something you should learn to do."

I rolled my eyes.

"It is seriously impossible to talk to you."

"So, what made you two start talking? You have a class together? Did you approach him first? No, no that's stupid... But it doesn't really make sense the other way around..."

"It's complicated," I responded, holding back my desire to lash out at her unnecessary comments. My face grew hot, and my hands shook in the anger that coursed through me.

"Well, you hold on to him now, you hear. You wait too long, and the good ones will be gone. If you've got a good one, never let him go."

Silence fell between us as she took out her phone and typed at lightning speed, no doubt already spreading information to Tom and my sister. I sighed and looked about the restaurant, taking in the scenery, observing the people. My stomach rumbled at every plate of food that landed on the table of others, despite the taste of orange smoothie still lingering in my mouth.

Our plates arrived and I started to eat right away. My mom stared at her plate then at her phone. After a moment, she took a picture of her food, typed out some text, then sat still, staring at her plate for another minute. Her phone sounded and she read a message and sent a response. Setting her phone down once more, she scraped out any sauce that was inside of her wrap, along with the shreds of cheese, leaving no more than chicken strips, tomato, and lettuce. With a sigh, my mom took a bite and shivered.

"Is that really gonna fill you up?" I asked, upset with the direction she seemed to be headed.

"Oh, yes," she forced a smile and showed me a thumbs up. "It's delicious and super nutritional."

"Mom, I just want your opinion. What makes some one 'one of the good ones?'"

"Well, being attractive doesn't hurt," she giggled, patting at her lip with a napkin. "But I think someone who values your time and listens to how you feel is also very important. Being able to talk things through, now that's a tricky one to find in a guy. You find someone who would rather talk than fight, just know you found a keeper. I haven't ever found one of those, but I've been told they're out there."

"Would you ever choose being with a good guy over hanging with your best friend? Like what if, hypothetically, I've got two things going on and I have to choose one?"

"Well, I would think both the good guy and the best friend should respect your decision either way. But I haven't had friends in decades," a tragic laugh found its way from her, her hand quickly rising up as she cleared her throat and scratched at the tip of her nose. "If it were me, I would go with the guy, especially if he's a keeper. Like I said, they're just too rare to pass up. Especially if he's cute."

Her response ended with a wink.

I bit my lip and thought about her words. I wanted to make tomorrow work, to make every day moving forward work. But any time with him would take away from Jordyn and I and any time with her would take away from Chase and me. My head spun as I felt like I needed to make a choice between them. Of all people, I probably shouldn't be taking advice from my mom, but I had no one else to turn to. Isn't that what mothers are for?

I finished my sandwich, wiped my greasy fingers on a napkin, and picked up my phone. I saw messages from both Jordyn and Chase asking to hang out later. I gulped. Having to make a choice was going to happen sooner than I expected.

Chapter Fourteen

My mom and I left the restaurant and, after the most awkward departing hug one could possibly imagine, I trudged back to my dorm. I rubbed my fingers against my phone in my pocket, not wanting to pull it out and have to send an answer to one or the other. I would feel less guilty telling both of them I was busy, but not only was that a blatant lie, I would be taking away time I could be spending with him.

Chase could never replace Jordyn, I knew that, but he did fill a piece of my heart that sat empty for so long. It was new, it was exhilarating. I wanted to reach that point of being bored of his hugs, of choosing food over his kisses, of swatting him away from an affectionate moment because I just wasn't feeling it. But none of those emotions or thoughts existed now. I wanted more, I craved for it. I was obsessed, yes, that's what it was, and I didn't care. I didn't want an intervention. I wanted to be with him until it was no longer the only thing I could think about.

I paused on the sidewalk, the point of no return. I stood at approximately the halfway point between his dorm and my own. I tapped my finger against my phone screen, the pressure of my teeth biting down on my lip growing painful. Why lie to myself any further? I knew which choice I wished to make. After having sat through a torturous meal with my mom, I just wanted to relax and feel loved by someone.

Removing my phone from my pocket, I texted Chase.

I'm good now. Where do you want to meet?

I pulled up Jordyn's messages and read through. Most of them were her still panicking about her poem, but also about how she discovered a new favorite band that was going to start playing at The Lounge. I giggled as I read through her erratic texts, never seeming to have a point and all over the place with random emojis thrown in.

I'm busy with something right now, but I'll be available later. You want me to meet you at the Lounge tonight?

I clicked send and she responded before Chase did.

Yes yes yes

I laughed and felt better. Guilt ate away at my stomach as I tried to convince myself I wasn't abandoning her for him. I could make this work. I wanted to more than anything.

He opened the door into his dorms and led me up the stairs. The guys' dorm definitely smelled different than ours, and the walls on either side of the hallway could use some extra cleanings, maybe under a black light. He led me into his room, his roommate already gone for the weekend.

"He flies home like every week. I mean, if you've got the money, right?"

"I don't know," I stated, my eyes wandering the space. "I came here to escape home. Unfortunately, part of it found its way here today."

"How did it go? That thing with your mom?"

"Oh, you know, she threw some insults, slashed away at my self-confidence, tried to give advice that really wasn't so bad, but let's be honest, she'll never be a therapist," I sighed and sat at the edge of the bed as he patted it in a gesture for me to take a seat. "I just... I wanted to believe that she'd change. That we could see eye to eye for once. But I don't think that's ever going to happen."

"You can't change people. They have to decide that for themselves. They have to make that jump."

"I guess you're right. She'll just try to fit into whatever mold her new boyfriend wants."

Chase laughed. His hand found my thigh, and he stared at my face. Our eyes connected, his glittering despite the low light of the room.

"I would never expect you to change for me," he whispers reassuringly.

I smile and place a hand on his.

"I appreciate that."

"I mean, if I wasn't like attracted to you, I probably wouldn't have kissed you in the first place."

I scoffed, thinking back to our time, close and contained, in the closet. A mockery of a game became a turning point in my life. A kiss that changed the course of my life. My finger traced the veins of his hand, his muscles tensing as I did so.

His other hand rose to turn my cheek, our faces almost touching. I felt the warmth of his breath pass my lips. We gave in to the other's weakness. My hand combed through the hair at the back of his head, then ran down to his shoulder folding inward as it landed above his pounding heart. I could feel it racing, wondering if his heart did no more than mock mine as it pounded away in my ears. We fell sideways into his blankets, our lips never parting.

I transcended time as his hand rubbed up and down my waist to my hip. I tried not to concentrate too hard on how I kissed, wanting it to seem natural and unforced. His lips moved fluidly with mine, thinking of him having plenty of practice was definitely not the distraction I wanted from my own insecurities.

After several minutes we parted, both of us releasing a dazed, giggly exhale as we rotated to our backs. We stared at the ceiling, smiling as if seeing something more than just the faded white paint.

"You ever just think that the future is already made for us."

I turned to him and propped my head up.

"What do you mean?"

He continued to stare at the ceiling.

"Like, what if all of this was meant to happen? What if you were meant to room with Sara, and I was meant to date her for a bit, just so we could meet each other and eventually kiss? What if it all had to perfectly align for us to be here, right now?"

"Are you high?" I joked. My hand moved to the sleeve of this shirt, rubbing the fabric between my fingers.

He sat up and turned to me.

"I just never imagined feeling this way."

"You literally just broke up with someone you felt comfortable enough saying you loved. What could you possibly be feeling that erases all of that?"

He bit his lip and grabbed the edge of his bed.

"You're never going to let me forget, right? Can't we just let go of the past?"

"Is it really that easy to admit you love someone and then break it off the next day?"

"That relationship was never serious to begin with."

"And what makes this," I pointed my finger between us in quick succession. "What makes this serious?"

"Well, I mean, we both have the same feelings, right?"

"And?"

"A relationship is two-sided. If one side isn't there, it doesn't matter what the other feels. If they never get that love back, love will never happen."

I choked back the first words to rise in my head, wanting to believe it wasn't true. I sat up and pulled my legs to my chest, scrunched my nose, not knowing what to say next.

His sigh was powerful enough to echo from the walls, filling the room with an irritated air.

"Listen, I just wanted to cheer you up after that awful thing with your mom. I didn't think we would be talking about all of this again." His hands landed on my shoulders and massaged them in a gentle, playful manner. "Why can't you just relax a bit?"

I resigned to his words and collapsed into his arms. His hands moved to my hair as my head rested on his chest.

"I'll be honest," he whispered, peering down at me with a grin. "I'm surprised you feel so comfortable being so close. I thought you'd be more distant. Surprised but not disappointed."

I sat up and reciprocated his smile. It was forced. His words almost hit me with a painful sting. I instantly thought of my mom. How quickly and carelessly she fell in love time and time again. A chill traveled up my spine. To think in any way I would have adopted her obsessive personality, her constant desire for affection and approval. It all hit me in a surreal wave. I jumped up from the bed.

"So," I searched for words, wanting to distract from these intrusive thoughts. "Besides soccer, what else do you like to do?"

He leaned forward, elbows on his knees and hands swiping his hair back, the muscles of his forearms caught the light just right. I almost caved and fell back into him.

"Well, I like hanging out with friends, watching movies."

"Ooh, what kind of movies?"

"Action and fighting ones. The funny ones are cool, too."

"What else?"

"I like..." his eyes scanned the room, as if he was really interested in no more than the three things listed. "Um, well, I like watching soccer. And, really not much else. I guess I'm kind of boring now that I think about it."

I bit my lip as I crossed my arms, wondering how our differences would ever work out.

"And what about you?"

"I enjoy reading and studying. I enjoy hanging out with Jordyn."

"That's the crazy one that hangs out with you sometimes, right?"

"That's a bit unnecessary, isn't it? She's just energetic and entertaining. No need to bash her for it."

"Sorry, sorry. Didn't mean to offend," Chase said with an uncomfortable laugh.

I bit my lip and committed to a deep breath.

"And you like drawing, too, right?"

"Yea," I mumbled, "I do."

"I know I already told you, but that's super cool. It takes someone with super talent to be an artist."

The corner of my mouth rose, the slight temptation to smile relaxing my tensed muscles. He must have sensed my tension because he stood and wrapped his arms about me. His hands gently pushed at my arms to rotate me to face him. He leaned forward to whisper into my ear.

"I'm so happy you're here with me."

The butterflies flew about my stomach and my emotions bounced from one extreme to another. I debated whether he toyed with me or if it was all real. I took a deep breath as I buried my head into his chest. As I rested there, I listened to his heart, erratic and anxiously it beat. Pressing closer to him, I knew he wasn't lying. Perhaps his words were no more than sweet talk, but there was some level of attraction there.

My face turned upward, my eyes inviting him in. Our lips met and none of my thoughts mattered anymore. I was lost to time and space. No doubt that my mind could invent would ever be able to push past the temptation of his affection.

Our lips parted but a lingering breath was shared between us as we hesitated to pull apart. Physicality was surely our love language, as his words never made me feel as secure as his embrace and his kisses. His gentle, warm touch was the equivalent of wrapping a blanket about myself on a cold day. Safe and secure. No desire to move or leave the comfort. I wanted our words to find that same space, share that bond. Communication seemed to be the failure in most relationships, or so my dad told me that was what went wrong between him and my mother. But maybe I was rushing. Maybe that took time.

"Wanna watch a movie or something?"

I answered with a smile and a nod. Chase rushed to turn on the television and pull up the streaming app, perhaps thinking I would change my mind.

"This one look good?"

The icon hovered over a decades-old kung fu movie. I released a breathy laugh and nodded again.

He selected the movie and threw the control to the side. With a playful grin, Chase lifted me from the floor, sweeping my legs into his arm, and tossed me onto his bed. The shock and fun of it all sent me into a fit of laughter. He jumped beside me and wrapped an arm about me. His chest pressed against my back, his arm securing me there. His other hand adjusted my hair so he could lay his head near mine.

"I could never play like that with Sara," were his last words before the movie started.

The saliva built up in my mouth so fast I could barely keep myself from choking on it as I tried to gulp down my nerves. I didn't want to ask what he meant, nor did I want to return to talking about his time with Sara. I thought we had moved past it. I thought he wanted to forget. Perhaps he'd never be able to.

When the movie finished, I promptly left, with no more than a kiss and a hug. He reminded me of the party the next night, wondering what time we wanted to head out. I told him I'd get back to him later. There was no way I wanted to stick around, so many thoughts and words wanting to spill from my mouth. If the doubts never left, why did I want to be by his side so badly?

I texted Jordyn as soon as I left the dorm.

Are you already at the Lounge?

I headed that way anyways, knowing she'd show up eventually.

What do you think

I expected no differently from her.

The chilly air forced my arms to wrap about myself to keep in my body heat and whatever residual heat signature he had left on me. Chase definitely knew how to make a lasting impression, in more ways than one. Unfortunately, that wasn't always a good thing. When we kissed, it was like I never wanted to forget, his impression lingering there until the next time we did so again. But his words... they held a different weight in my mind. I always wondered if I was just misinterpreting him, if I was making something out of nothing. Did my mind force any intention into his words that wasn't really there?

My pace quickened as the cold bit through my jacket and pants. At least I could relax my tense nerves once I got there, knowing that I succeeded in what I aimed to do. I could maintain both relationships, I could find time for both of them. It eased my doubts for the next day.

I didn't have to choose.

I could have both and be happy.

But was I truly happy with both?

Chapter Fifteen

The next morning, I searched through my closet as I ate breakfast. None of my clothes gave off a partying vibe. In honesty, my entire closet gave off the vibe of an anxious college freshman without the luxury of a parent's charge card. Most of my clothes were what still fit me from high school, my style being dull, or as Jordyn put 'subtle earthy tones'. I appreciated her optimism, nonetheless.

Sara and Bridgette entered with a huge box of bagels, donuts, and more coffee than the two of them should drink in one morning.

"Having a breakfast party?" I asked, praying that no more from their group would actually be coming over.

"Uh, no," Sara answered, in a tone that stated she did not appreciate my comment. She eyed the food then peered down at herself, wondering the conclusion that others would draw had they witnessed the same thing. She shrugged it off and grabbed a bagel.

"We have to find our outfits for the party tonight."

A pit dropped in my stomach. My eyes connected with Sara's as she took a bite of a cinnamon crunch bagel, her satisfied moan issued as a taunt to me. Bridgette stepped to Sara's closet and swiped the hangers back and forth as she struggled to hold back the multitudes of clothes to get a good look at every dress or outfit within.

"Roger and Dean are hosting at their frat house, so you know it's gonna be a good time," Sara said as she winked at me and set her bagel down.

"Sounds like fun."

I shut my closet door and slid the tops I had placed on my bed to the side. My eyes moved to my phone, trying to ignore the fashion show happening in front of me. Bridgette, who was luckily the same size as Sara, shopped in her friend's closet for something to wear as well.

They kept mumbling about their bodies, their insecurities about themselves just going to show that not even the prettiest are made to feel secure about themselves. As they kept going back and forth about the drama that might start and who might be there, my ears perked up at the sound of his name.

"You think Chase will be there?" Bridgette asked, as if looking to rile up her friend.

It didn't seem to work. Sara nonchalantly flipped her hair to the side and observed herself in a short, knit dress in the mirror.

"I mean, probably. Dean and him are like best friends almost."

"Wow," Bridgette sat on the bed next to a pile of clothes they had tried on and deemed not worthy. "He's probably gonna crack when he sees you and Roger together. You think he'll try to fight him or something?"

"I mean, maybe," Sara said as she undressed and threw another dress atop the pile. "But Roger is so much stronger than him. He'll just take him out. He'll probably start crying or something, just like when I broke up with him."

My brow furrowed, but I quickly shook the expression hoping they hadn't noticed. Not that they would mind if I joined in on their gossip. They would probably love to add to their circle of drama, having another just validate anything and everything they say. It seemed that all people wanted were friends that were echo chambers. Granted, my mom tried that time and time again with her new love interests, turns out people just get bored with that after a while.

"Oh yes!" Sara jumped up and down as she twirled and admired her reflection in the mirror. She wore a tattered pair of high waisted shorts with a graphic tank and cardigan. "This is perfect!"

"You look so cute!" Bridgette leapt up from the bed and pretended to snap pictures of her best friend.

Sara made gestures in the mirror after pulling out her own phone and snapping some pics. Bridgette joined beside her, and they hugged and swayed as they stuck out their tongues and made peace signs at the camera. The longer I sat there watching them, the more I realized how different I was from Sara. I was either not Chase's type at all, or he had guessed totally wrong about Sara's type when they were together.

My guess, and that answer that had been clouding my thoughts since day one, was that Chase assumed me to be more like Sara than was actually true. Sure, we were roommates. Sure, we spoke sometimes. But there were far more differences than similarities between us than I could count on both hands and feet.

Bridgette, who had already found her dress, rushed to put it on and take pictures of herself in the mirror as Sara indulged in another bagel. Once they both felt they were the best they were going to get, they decided to take off to get their nails done.

"If you want a bagel or donut, take one," Sara offered to me as she closed the door.

"Thanks," I mumbled. My stomach growled as if shouting at me to take up her offer, but I couldn't help but feel eating something offered to me by her would surely poison me, whether actually or just some placebo effect.

I stood at my closet and pulled out my drawers, examining my options. I tried to pay as best attention to what they tried on in my peripheral vision, their fashion sense the only way I had a chance at wearing something trendy. I pulled out a pair of skinny jeans with intentional ripping on the thighs and knees. I never wore them because I always felt kind of out of my element in them. However, I would already feel out of my element at a party, so might as well try to blend in as much as possible. I noticed a graphic tee with a superhero emblem on the front and glanced at a navy cardigan hanging up. I bit my lip and debated. After some thought, and not wanting to appear too much like her should Chase actually start to believe some made up claim of our similarities, I grabbed a sequined tank top and fashion blazer (that my mom bought me for my final in oral communications in high school) and threw them on my bed.

I didn't want to waste too much energy on this, just thinking about the party already draining me. I'd want to sleep before even getting there if it kept up.

My phone vibrated and I raced to see the message.

I'm freaking out! It's almost time! Do you really think it's good enough? I'm so nervous!!

I released a breathy laugh as I read Jordyn's texts. One after another. Her lack of self-confidence almost made me feel like I could take on the world. And, as a best friend should, I was her echo chamber, telling her exactly what she needed to hear.

You're gonna do great! I'll be there to cheer you on!

Another message popped through.

Hey, you. You wanna get lunch?

It was Chase. I fought to catch my breath, seeing a message from him causing me more nerves than being there beside him. It still felt like a dream. As I woke up every morning, I didn't believe it until I saw him again the next day. When he would hug me, kiss me, speak sweet words to me, my mind always wandered to the possibility of it being some sick prank.

Let's do it. You want me to head over there?

I'll come get you.

And every time, no matter my doubts, I gave in.

Not knowing if we'd be returning after, I put on my party outfit and headed to the lounge below to wait for him. As I opened the door to exit, he quickly grabbed it from my hand and led me out. He wrapped an arm about my shoulder and pulled me in for a kiss on the cheek.

"Always so romantic?" I giggled, leaning into his chest.

"What are you talking about? That's not being romantic. I'm just happy to see you."

Chase laughed and we walked to a buffet for our lunch. He grabbed one of my hands into his pocket and worked it from my glove, lacing his fingers with mine. Every breath created a mist in front of our faces, every laugh causing my face to grow more red. He spoke and I listened. His jokes were funny, always having a commentary on everything. From the tales of his week at soccer practice and their next game coming up, to something ridiculous a fellow classmate said on their online forum, his stories seemed to never end. I envied his ability to talk so fluidly, as if it took so little thought. I wondered if he ever managed to get in a word with Sara, though, he always seemed much quieter when they were together.

I took my coat off when we got to our booth, removing any other unnecessary winter accessories along with it. His eyes scanned my body and a grin spread across his face.

"You look super nice. Did you do that for the party, or just for me?"

The question was a trap. I knew it was.

"Well, obviously for you," I laughed, brushing my frizzy hair from my face as it fought to hold to my headband. "Not like I'm hoping to hook up with anyone at the party. I've already got everything I need right in front of me."

He bit his lip and nodded, his eyes not leaving mine.

"Let's, uh, get something to eat."

We filled our plates with the best an Italian buffet could offer, pastas and breads, anything and everything coming with a variety of tomato and garlic. The smell of the place was divine, the food even better.

Even as we ate, the same thought kept striking me until I could no longer ignore it.

"Um, Chase," I started, wanting to pull his attention so I didn't have to repeat myself. "You do know that Sara's gonna be at that party tonight, right?"

His face didn't express the shock I thought it would. Rather, his eyes turned back to his plate, and he shrugged.

"I figured, I mean, it is her new man that's hosting the thing."

"And you don't mind that? Being seen there? With me?"

"Don't be stupid," he laughed before the grin dropped to a frown and he shook his head urgently. "I'm sorry, I didn't mean to say it like that."

"So, you don't care about being seen with me?"

"Absolutely not."

He set down his fork and knife and reached both hands across the table. They cupped my hand that no more than sat there holding my napkin. His fingers rubbed across the back of my hands, his caress more forceful than gentle as his expression hardened. He appeared as if even he debated what to say, as if he was just going with the motions, not thinking too much about what could happen next.

"Listen," he started, still rubbing my hands and refusing eye contact while he spoke. "If I really cared about being seen with you, don't you think I'd hide all of this a bit better. Honestly, it's been a bit lucky she hasn't figured it out yet."

"Lucky?"

"I didn't mean it like that."

"Then how did you mean it?"

"Like, lucky that you haven't been put into an awkward situation yet. I'd rather talk to her about it than force you to. I've dealt with her before. I know how to handle her."

"But why does it matter? You broke up with her, right? Like you two are not a thing, no longer talking. I'm getting it right, right?"

"Yeah, totally."

He pulled his hands back and started cutting at his pork Milanese again. I couldn't eat and just stared at my plate. Chase noticed within seconds and sighed.

"Please, just hear me out. Sara and I are not together. I'm allowed to be with whoever I want. I chose you. That should make you happy, right?"

The way he said it stung in a way I don't think he intended. When not in romantic scenarios like holding hands or in an embrace, his words felt cold. His tone wasn't icy, just as nonchalant as any college guy when talking about feelings, I guess. I know we only recently started dating, but I wondered if hiding a softer part of him was some defense mechanism. As if bringing up Sara's name was enough to go on the defensive. Had it hurt so bad to break up with her? Or was being in a relationship with her what broke him?

I finally picked up my fork and poked at the lasagna on my plate, cutting it into tiny bites in hopes I wouldn't choke on it as my thoughts distracted me. And, bite after bite, a new message came through on my phone. I moved my finger to my pocket and clicked to button to turn it from vibrations to silence.

Jordyn's nerves were contagious. Her anxiety leaked and I was absorbing every bit that came to me.

"I just have to get through the party," I mumbled. "Just get through the party."

Chapter Sixteen

I cleared my plate for the first time as he ate away at his second round of food. Judging by his pace, he was going for a third round as well. Unlike me, those carbs would burn away come his next practice for soccer. I'd be lucky to burn off the carbs of a lasagna noodle walking back to the dorm.

God, my mom has messed me up so much...

We finished our meals and sat there a bit longer, not wanting to walk in the cold too soon after filling our stomachs.

"Party starts in a few hours. Wanna catch a movie back at my place?"

I accepted the invitation, and we took off.

My brain was as full as my stomach. Once on his bed, I wanted to sleep and wake up the next day, hoping that someone who could pass as me would go to the party with Chase and attend Jordyn's reading. I couldn't take the stress, the mental and physical toll it was taking on me far exceeding even my worries of exams. Rather than watch the movie, my eyes stared past the screen, the words catching my ears were unrecognizable. I zoned out and allowed my mind to go blank, as best I could.

After several minutes, an arm wrapped about me. It pulled me in, hardened muscles pressing against my side and my waist as it gently adjusted my position. A hand caught my cheek, turning my head slightly upward. Gentle lips met the corner of my mouth. The pressure holding my back upright disappeared, and I moved to lay flat on the bed. He hovered over me and leaned into another kiss.

Mindless and senseless, my arms wrapped about his neck. I held him there. Not that he struggled to be released. For, as much as I held him to position, he did the same to me.

Time passed and our lips parted. He placed his head on my shoulder and kept an arm about my waist. Before long, his breathing changed pace, taking longer and deeper breaths. I glanced over to see his eyes closed. My eyes peered at the television, wondering if it would disturb his sleep. The longer I debated, the drowsier I grew. I decided my sudden movement would wake him. My eyelids threatened to close, and I fought as best I could. I lost the battle.

When I woke up, the television had gone black to inactivity. I checked my phone and freaked out at the time. The party had started over an hour ago. Chase slept without a worry, lost to his dream world, relaxed, peaceful. I questioned whether I even wanted to wake him. I didn't want to go to that party anyways. But he did. I sighed.

"Chase, Chase," I called to him in a whisper, not wanting to startle him. My attempts didn't work as he flinched awake.

"What?" he groggily asked as he wiped at his eyes.

"The party. Are we still going?"

"Oh shit."

He jumped up, grabbed his phone, and cursed again. Catching his reflection, he tossed his hair in a mirror and looked to me.

"How long before you're ready to go?"

"I mean, I've kind of been ready."

He laughed and shook his head. I knew he made another comparison to Sara of our different habits.

"Then let's get going."

We bundled up and ran down the street, the music in the distance already reaching our ears. A crowd of students were out on the front lawn, cups with indistinguishable drinks in hand. As we passed to enter the frat house, Chase wrapped an arm about me, holding me close, whether for my sake or his own.

His supposed friends waved and nodded as we passed. With his free hand, he shared a handshake with some of them, unable to do that manly handshake hug thing due to me being in his other arm. Chase didn't seem to care.

I was met with odd looks by some of them. Whispers started and I figured the drama and gossip were already brewing. I held my breath as we passed through a cloud of smoke, having never gotten used to the smell despite one of my mom's ex boyfriends having been a chain smoker. As we walked through the front door, a word of gossip made it to my ears.

"That must be the rebound since Sara dumped him. Wonder what Roger's gonna say."

I gulped. Chase told me one story, but everyone else seemed to believe another. Sara's just spreading shit, I tried to convince myself. She was distraught that night, totally caught off guard. She just wanted to take control of the situation, seem like she was the one making the call.

My train of thought could not continue without interruption as the crowd in the house made movement almost impossible. You couldn't slip past someone without touching the back of another. I was not built for this type of environment.

Chase switched from having his arm wrapped about me to holding my hand. Not that I felt there was any less chance of me losing him like this. I was in sensory overload. People laughed, screamed, talked, music blared. Sweaty, smelly college students and their overpowering colognes and perfumes mixed to create a rancid scent within the house, though some of that smell may have existed before the party even started. The walls were stained, the carpets a mess. I refused to touch anything, keeping my hands as near to me as possible.

He pulled me through the house, and we ended up in the dining area. The crowd was sparse in this part, many of them standing out in the chill of the backyard as their bodies numbed to the temperature.

The open concept made the kitchen visible, a mess of appetizers and pizzas on an island in the center.

"Chase, bro, what's up?"

A man with a brown military cut but bleached sides walked over to us. He wore a football jersey and appeared the most sober one at the moment. The two shared a handshake that pulled into a quick embrace.

"Yo, Dean. What's going on? Things look sick. Great turn out."

"Yeah, more than I expected. Word gets out and it's over."

Dean glanced at me with a smile, nodding in hello, then caught Chase's eyes for a moment.

"This is Alex. She's with me."

"Yeah..."

Dean held out the word for longer than made me comfortable. I could feel his hesitation in making any formal introduction, as if unsure which side of the drama he fell into. He glanced outside for a moment, then back to me, offering a hand.

"Nice to meet you, Alex. I hope you're treating my man right. He's a good guy."

"She is," Chase interjected right away, before my jaw could even drop to answer. "She's super talented, super smart, super pretty. Anything anyone could hope for. I'm a lucky guy."

I saw Dean bite his lip just before turning my eyes to the ground. His eyes crawled over me, as if trying to see what Chase saw in me. I didn't understand his defensiveness, as if he was preparing for the drama and gossip to meet him in the coming days, or in the next couple of minutes.

"I'm happy for you two. Enjoy the party and try to avoid the backyard."

He winked at Chase and clicked his tongue before heading off. Chase and I both glanced out the door and saw her. A pit dropped into my stomach. I felt the desire to vomit. Sara, drink in one hand, new guy in the other, laughed and joked in a circle of friends. Bridgette had two guys, one at each arm, taking a turn sipping from their drinks. Their pleasure of attention and the high they got from it made me understand even more so why I was not a party person.

Chase cleared his throat and pulled out a chair for me at the dining table.

"Let's just sit and relax."

I nodded and took a seat, not that I could refuse because my legs felt like gelatin. He pulled out another chair and took a seat next to me. As soon as he sat, he leaned down with his elbows on his knees, biting at his thumb. I think his instructions were more so for himself than for me.

"So, how do you know Dean?" I asked, attempting to distract his mind.

"Buddy of mine. His younger brother plays soccer with us. They're both good friends."

"You know a lot of the others here?"

"Just their faces, not their names. They hang out with this group only when a party happens. Probably weren't even invited, just caught word of it."

I licked my lips, my eyes scanning the room at everything happening around. A group of guys went into the kitchen, scavenged through the scraps left in the boxes, and returned to a group of ladies while swallowing the last bits of food they could chew, claiming there was no food left. No one really danced to the music, it was more so just to block out the noise of rowdy drunks unable to form full sentences. At least half in attendance were of legal age, the cops probably didn't even want to waste their time unless the group became too much of a ruckus. University frat houses weren't quite known for their housing of saints.

Before I could warn him, she walked through the door and cleared her throat. Chase glanced up and frowned. Rather than address him, her eyes found me.

"What are you doing here?" Sara asked. She crossed her arms and squinted, eyes moving between Chase and me.

"I invited her," Chase spoke, again, without giving me even the chance of an opportunity to speak.

Sara released a breathy chuckle. Bridgette's laugh announced her presence before she made it to Sara's side. Her smile instantly dropped when she saw us together.

"What the eff..."

"Oh, let me explain," Sara said, her face serious. "He invited her here. Poor thing."

Bridgette barred her teeth as if expressing the awkwardness of the situation that we refused to acknowledge. My face grew flushed as my internal temperature rose. I wanted to race outside. I wanted to run back to the dorms, hide under my covers. I didn't even want his embrace to help me feel better, as if just seeing him would force the memories to resurface.

"Chase, I was told to come and get you. Dean and Roger need some help out back. Do you mind?"

Chase sighed and stood up, not thinking twice about following her orders. I gulped, not understanding his voluntarily putting me into this situation. Sara and Bridgette smirked as he walked past but didn't move from their positions.

"Just so you know," Sara spoke to me, her tone lighter than before. "I don't care that you're with him. That's fine. You do you. Just know that he tries to manipulate and control your emotions. He doesn't actually care. He'll tell you all the sweet things you want to hear, but he doesn't mean any of it."

She sighed and rubbed at her manicure, long nails with bright shades of pink and gold glitter.

"I'm so glad I dumped him for Roger. Roger is so much hotter, stronger, and he actually cares about me. He treats me like the queen

I am. And you," she pointed at me, "shouldn't settle for anyone who treats you any less than royalty."

Sara waited a moment, then, realizing I wasn't going to respond, strutted away with Bridgette at her heels.

I let out the breath I had been holding in and felt a fraction of relief. To hear her say she didn't care I was with him was a huge weight lifted off, especially given that at the end of the night we would still be roommates. But while my relationship with her appeared to stabilize, her words filled me with worry about how I felt about Chase.

Maybe she was right. He always spoke sweet words when we were in an affectionate moment, but every time after just seemed bland. Had I hoped for too much? Imagining some fairytale love story that wasn't a reality, would never be a reality? Did I put too much pressure on him to be perfect while I still had so many flaws?

Chase returned with a cup in hand and sat down at my side. He wrapped an arm about me and offered me a drink. I shook my head and looked to the ground. He sighed.

"I'm sorry to abandon you like that. Just that I owe Dean a lot. He's helped me through a lot, and I just got to help when he needs me."

"It's fine," I mumbled, refusing to look up.

Because I wouldn't, his hand forced me as it cupped my chin and lifted my head. He kissed my forehead and offered me a drink again.

"It's just orange soda. It's not gonna hurt you. I promise."

I stared at the contents of the cup for a couple of seconds before finally giving in. The sweet soda quenched a thirst I didn't realize I had.

"Thanks," I said, giving the cup back to him.

We sat in silence, the crowd inside thinning out as the students went outside for drinks and smoking. I played with the sequins on my top, not knowing what else to do.

"This was an awful idea. I'm sorry to put you through this. I just thought, you know, Sara liked it. Sara loves this kind of stuff. Thought maybe you would too. I guess I just should have listened better."

His realization struck as genuine caring. His words weren't toxic, they weren't malicious, and he wasn't trying to sweet talk. His tone was sincere. His words were an attack of his own shortcomings and mistakes.

With a deep inhale and a new light shining in my eyes, I leaned in and kissed his cheek. His eyes reflected that which shone from mine, a smile crossing his face.

"Don't be too hard on yourself. You said you also like these things. Even if it is just to people watch. We can do that together."

Chase giggled and set his empty cup on the table.

"You're right." He nudged my arm and pointed toward a pair. "That's the second girl he's been trying to get tonight. His actual girl isn't even here, probably went home for the weekend or something."

I grinned and glanced about.

"Ooh," I gasped and nodded my head in the direction. Chase pulled me nearer, almost excited that I was as invested in the game as he was. "Look at her hair. Isn't it just perfect? Long, perfectly executed French braid. You're going to have to learn how to do that for me."

We both laughed. Our hands nestled into one another, and our eyes searched for our next targets. Before long, my gaze wandered out the door. I noticed Sara tucking some guy's hair behind his ear, her finger then sliding from his shoulder to his forearm before circling the rim of her cup. Dean and Roger weren't far from the scene, both working to prop up some outdoor lights on a post. As my eyes found Dean, he caught them and made a gesture to get Chase's attention.

I snapped from the game and bumped Chase.

"I think Dean needs you again."

I pointed and Chase's eyes followed.

"I'll be right back," he said with a sigh.

Waiting in silence felt much better than being abandoned in the company of Sara. Despite the drama I thought would ensue, she seemed rather collected about the whole situation. Maybe she had been as ready to move on as Chase when they finally split.

I scanned the kitchen and living room area, the smells lingering grew more powerful by the second, people walking in and out understandably trying to dodge being stuck in the scent. The volume of the music had decreased indoors as it no longer fought to overpower people and their conversations. My foot tapped along to some emo rock song that started playing, my head bobbing as I checked to see if Chase was almost done.

My heart sank. A cramp worse than any my cycles could have given me hit in an instant. My throat closed and I felt I couldn't breathe even if I wanted to.

Chase, back facing me, held a post while Dean climbed a ladder. Roger walked past me in the dining room, heading to who-knows-where, leaving Chase and Dean to do the task themselves. But what caused the lump to grow in my throat was her presence at his side. He stood there, unmoving, laughing at her jokes as she spoke to them both. Her hand fell on his shoulder and worked her way down his bicep, squeezing at his muscle and tracing every bit of curve with her finger. His expression didn't appear to care, quite the opposite.

Little did I know the worst part was to come.

Her hand moved back up his arm to play with the hair on the back of his head. After a few twirls, her hand slid down his back and rested there, comfortable and at home. It was so natural, as something she had done countless times before.

Sara leaned in and whispered in his ear. Chase turned and giggled along with her.

Of everything I could throw, of everyone I could blame, of every curse I could say, my heart restricted it all. The tears formed and all I could think to do was stand and run from the space before I had to face him. I didn't actually run, I didn't want to bring more attention to myself. My stupid self. Of all the stupid things I wanted to make for myself, make for my future, I ended up with the one fate I tried to avoid. I had turned into my mom.

So desperate for love. So desperate for affection. I saw her lose the game time and time again. I could see it come from a mile away every time no matter how she chose to ignore it. And when the waterworks would flow, I'd be the shoulder she would cry on. Maybe that's why she resented me. I reminded her of all the times she was weak.

I walked down the street, embracing myself to keep in the heat. I hoped that even if I froze, no one would be able to uncross my arms and see the hole my heart escaped from. It hadn't escaped yet. I would know if it had for the beating and pummeling, its constant attack on my chest and every blood vessel it used to emit its angry pulse through the rest of my body would be sure to let me know it was gone. I would be dead before the bruising of its last beat formed. The heart, the imagery for love and romance, was in this moment no more than a reminder of my rage and the violent urges that coursed through me.

But I was no victim. Not to my heart. Not to him.

I was stupid. I willingly put myself into that situation. Why did I do it? I should have said something. Just told him I wasn't interested in going. Then what? He would have probably spent all night with her. Was I a pawn of revenge yet again? Used as a way for him to get back, hoping to make her jealous?

I shook my head. I didn't want to think about it. I didn't want to remember anything. Seeing either of their faces would only cause the wound to reopen. I wanted it to scab over. To go away for good. I couldn't keep running back to the same thoughts. Tossing away any and all doubts because I loved the attention and the affection he offered.

Betrayal was the only word I could think of in the moment. I had no use for the petty games he and Sara played. I wasn't interested. They could have all the fun they wanted. I just wanted to move on with my life. Get my degree. Escape into a life where I wasn't dependent on anyone but myself.

All I had was me. I was all I ever had.

Chapter Seventeen

I woke up the next morning with a roaring headache, cheeks sticky from the tear streams that dried there. My blankets were an unruly bundle that I fought to free myself from. I reached over the side of my bed and pulled up a pair of sweatpants laying on the floor. After getting dressed, I headed to the bathroom.

Early Sunday mornings were always so quiet. Most college students slept in until noon, others either relaxing in their dorm rooms or taking a morning jog. As I ripped through my knotty hair with a brush, I just stared at my reflection. My mind was blank. I cursed at the pain of tugging my hair from the bristles of the brush, letting it hang there when I needed my fingers to weave through the mess for a release. When I managed through the knots, left with a ball of frizz on my head, I sighed and turned to the showers. I felt gross and sticky and nasty. A shower would hopefully wash it all away.

Twenty minutes wasn't a long shower for many, but it was for me. The vapors clouded my vision as I turned the heat up, my feet red as the waters rushed past them to the drain. I shampooed once, twice, and then a third time. My muscles relaxed. I stood there and took deep breaths. When the waters of the arctic decided it was there time to enter the conversation, I quickly turned the knob and jumped from its path. I wrapped a towel around me and sat on a bench near my clothes.

I refused to think about the day, about what I was going to do next. I didn't want any thoughts to enter my mind. Blank. That's how I wanted it to remain. I didn't want to think. I didn't want to talk. I didn't want to do anything. Just sit there, in silence, and hope no one would come in to interrupt it.

My fingers fidgeted, picking at the sides of my fingernails as my thoughts pounded at the door like the water pushing against the dam in a storm. My headache was a distant drum beat after the shower, but I feared it would come back with a vengeance at any time. I dressed and returned my dirtied clothes to my room before going down to the lounge.

I sat on a sofa and put my headphones in, staring out the window as I started a new thriller. As always, it started from the perspective of an unknowing stranger about to find something they didn't want to see. The main character would then hear or see this witness account and somehow be pulled into the drama of the crime, the killer following their every footstep.

I pulled my knees to my chest and set my chin atop them. Despite going through my phone to get to the book, I did my best to ignore the endless notifications of missed messages. The top ones all had his face. My phone went on silent as soon as I hit the bed last night, waking up to it all not a way to start my day. So I put my phone on the cushion beside me and dove further into the narration of the story.

The sun refused to break through the clouds, vapor forming on the windows where the heater vents blew down to warm the space. My stomach grumbled, but I didn't want to meet the chill outside the doors. But I also didn't want to go up to my room for food. Sara would be waking up at any time, and I did not want a single interaction with her.

Just thinking her name cracked the dam holding back the waters as tears formed in my eyes. I covered my face with my arm, trying to hold them in, force them back. But my chest felt immense pressure, my head building up with the same. I allowed a few tears to slip by, hoping it would relieve that feeling. It wasn't enough. I swallowed my thoughts and emotions, smacked my cheeks a couple of times and walked out the door to the food court, with the hopes that a good breakfast sandwich could distract me before the inevitable explosion.

Sipping at the hot coffee forced bumps on my arms as it burned going down my throat. My shoulders hunched and I felt my neck stiffen. With a deep breath, I found the ability to relax. Despite my hesitation to do so, I turned on my phone screen, noticing another message had come through. I sighed and cleared the notifications.

As I went to take a bite of my sandwich, my stomach felt like it fell through the floor. A giant hole opened there and every muscle about it cramped. Thoughts were powerful, always able to manipulate the body to evoke the absolute worst response. Guilt was for sure the worst. As the thought struck, I felt every muscle in my body tense and the stress to hit my heart was enough to think I'd need hospitalized for a day or two. I couldn't believe it. I couldn't forgive myself. And worst of all, how would she ever forgive me?

I missed Jordyn's reading.

I slammed my head to the table, just barely missing my sandwich but enough that the melted cheese in the wrapper got into my hair. I didn't even care. Going straight to my messages, I found her highlighted bubble, so many missed ones.

When are you coming?

On ur way?

U okay?

Almost here?

It's almost time!!?!?

Wow...

And then silence. Nothing. I groaned.

Tapping my foot on the sticky tile, my eyes scanned the food court, as if hoping the perfect apology was written on the wall. How do I start? I didn't need bubbly words, I was no poet, and she more than knew that.

"Just be genuine," I mumbled and hovered my thumbs over the phone's keyboard. I took a deep breath.

I'm so sorry

The words were simple, yet they held every emotion racing through me in the most succinct way I could put it. It held the guilt, the pressure crushing me, not that it relieved me of any of those feelings. I was honestly shocked she hadn't blocked me yet.

I exited the app and stared at my home screen, not expecting an answer, but not entirely sure what to do next. His picture popped up as a call came through. With a hollow exhale, I quickly placed my phone face down on the table and grabbed my sandwich. With every bite, I felt my jaw struggling to chew as my entire body trembled. My arms quaked so badly I couldn't even place them on the tabletop.

I was the worst. The worst friend anyone could ever hope to have. He didn't even matter anymore. Every bit of the betrayal I felt from the night before turned to guilt for being the very thing I hated. I betrayed her. I abandoned her. I was so stupid.

Clearing off the table of my garbage and grabbing my things, I trudged from the food court aimlessly, not sure where I was going just letting my feet take me. I wandered to the library, hoping not many would choose the weekend to study. Ignoring all faces I passed, my feet led me to a solitary computer cubicle. Studying felt like the only thing I could do to pass the time. After several math problems, I grew bored. Solving equations for chemistry made me antsy. Reading independently on ancient civilizations, tools of debate, and themes in fiction made me depressed. There was no way I could mentally indulge myself in my classwork.

I turned on an audiobook and pulled out a notepad I kept in my purse. My pen circled across the page, making loop after loop. There was no rhyme or reason, just a stream of consciousness style of drawing. I let my hand guide me, having no care what images I created on the page. After several minutes, the ink smeared over the page and my hand, I pulled myself from the art and observed from afar. It was a dumpster fire. I literally drew a dumpster fire. Smoke, flames, a pile of garbage, it was all there. I sighed.

With a flip of the page, I took a deep breath and started writing. Again, it was stream of consciousness, but I dedicated my words to Jordyn. An apology. She would probably never see it. In honesty, I would probably tear it out and rip it into a million shreds as soon as I finished it, but it felt good to get it out.

Tears swelled in my eyes with every mistake, every stupid action I took and how I messed up. I signed the letter "Your Stupid Friend, Alex" and sat back to read what I'd written. It was rambly and some sentences made absolutely no sense. But it was real. It came from me. I was no poet. But every word mattered. And I meant every word that I said.

I stared at the computer until the screen fell asleep. The words of my book seemed to be going in one ear and out the other. I felt lost. I didn't know what to do.

My phone lit up again as a notification came through. I jumped, hoping it would be her. His face popped up, and I cleared the notification instantly. For lack of ideas, I scrolled through my phone's contacts wondering if there was anyone I could talk to, anyone I could turn to.

Reaching the end of the alphabet I paused and hovered over her contact. I had changed the name in years past after an argument, her name now displaying "Why is she my sister?". I licked my lips and pressed twice. The phone started ringing.

Scanning the library to ensure I wasn't bothering anyone that may be near, I waited with the phone to my ear, tapping my foot as I grew anxious. No one was around, yet it felt like a billion eyes watched me in confusion, wondering what I was going to say. Wondering how I could have fallen so low. The ringtone stopped and I heard a breath come through the phone.

"Hello?"

"Hey, Kelly. It's Alex, your sister."

"Yes, yes. Technology nowadays tells you who's calling. No need to introduce yourself, Alex, my sister."

Her dry sarcasm hit me differently than it had before. It was almost relaxing, reassuring. She was comfortable enough with me to be personable, put her personality behind the conversation and not take it too seriously. I thought I had burned my bridges, but this was perhaps the dash of hope I needed.

"It's weird for you to call. Is everything okay?"

"Yeah, I just, I need some advice and I figure it's better to ask you than mom."

"Uh oh. Must be some boy stuff. Yeah, mom's not the best with relationship advice, but you probably know that better than me. All those guys she brings home treat her like shit, and I know they treated you that way, too."

"I've been feeling really bad about it. Wanted to call you up a few times but figured you'd be too busy. All your schoolwork and college stuff and what not. I was never built for that stuff, just knew you would always be the one to succeed. I hoped so."

She went silent, her voice came across as more vulnerable, whether from a pressure she wished to get off her chest or the hormones from her pregnancy. Either way, I thanked whatever higher power was listening that I may have made the right choice, which seemed few and far between these days.

"You're right, well kind of. There's some boy stuff but also some friend stuff as well." I released an audible cry of exhaustion, surprising even me. "I just feel so stuck, and I have no idea what to do."

The dams threatened to break again. I hadn't had the chance to release the reservoirs yet and my time limit to do so was drawing near. If I pushed it much longer, I wouldn't have a choice of setting before they made that choice for me.

"Whoa whoa whoa, slow down. First off, always use a condom. Don't trust that other shit, trust me. Second, if this is about a boy *being* with your friend, drop them both so fast and run the other way."

"No, it's not that. None of that, thankfully. It's... I bit off more than I could chew. I thought I could have both a boyfriend and a best friend-"

"Uh, you definitely can."

"Okay, well I thought I could and well, if it's actually possible, I royally fucked up."

I told her what happened. Without interruption, without excuses or hesitation she listened. To every grueling moment, every cringey detail, she listened to it all. My sister, the only person I thought could be more critical of me, more spiteful than my mom, was the one to not only calm me down but actually listen.

"Have you tried talking to Jordyn?"

"I messaged her, but she hasn't responded back."

"Uh, you know people are actual beings right. Your phone doesn't just pop out a friend when it feels like it. Knock on her door. Talk to her."

"And have her punch me in the face? I know her well enough to know that nothing I could say would mean anything to her right now."

"Well, if she was really a friend, she would listen anyways, no matter how angry she was. I would be upset if you missed something like that sure, but more than that I would be worried sick because that is not the Alex I know."

"But-"

"I would have marched down to your room, ASAP, and tried to figure out what the hell happened. Sure, I would be angry after hearing your story. Shit, betrayed may be the right word, too. But people make mistakes."

"But when she needed me most, I wasn't there for her," I responded, biting my lip in anticipation of what my sister would say next.

"Shit, mom wasn't there for us and yet we still talk. I still check up to see how she's doing. I know that's different, she's family, but it's really not. Is Jordyn a baby? Is she some pet that depends on you for food and shelter? No. She's a grown-ass adult. And sometimes life doesn't go your way. Can't just throw a tantrum. She's got to get up and move on."

"But I don't want her to move on without me. I enjoy her company. I enjoy being her friend. I'm the one who messed up."

"Then tell her that."

I wanted to respond, to counter her point, but I couldn't. My sister was right. Jordyn and I would either find a way to make up or we'd both have to move on. My mouth hung open, unable to form words, not that I had any in mind to speak anyways. Heart rate calming after the rush of excitement, the dust settling after the storm, I let out a relieved exhale.

"I'll talk to her. If it doesn't work, it doesn't work."

"And if she really doesn't want to see you, you'll have to find another way to get her the message. She's hurt, I get it. Maybe words won't reach her. You might have to find another way. I'm sure you'll think of something."

"Yeah, there's got to be a way. By the way, how are you doing?"

"Oh, you know, still puking every morning. My current diet consists of chips and brownies, but I have to stack them on top of one another to get both the salt and sugar at the same time. I won't explain. You might understand one day."

I giggled and we ended our conversation in the most amicable way I could have imagined. With my head clear and the pressure lifting ever so slightly, it was time to put together a game plan.

My phone rang and his face appeared again. I scrunched my nose and stared at the screen.

Before I could focus on Jordyn, I had to deal with this.

Chapter Eighteen

Knowing I would cry, knowing I would scream, knowing I would say things I would probably regret with witnesses around, I gathered my belongings and marched out of the library. A cold day greeted me, no hopes of heating up as seasons changed. Barely any leaves remained on the trees, a crisp November breeze assuring us all of the snow right around the corner. I paused in the middle of the sidewalk. I had no idea where I should go now.

My eyes scanned about campus, wondering if there was a place, somewhere that would offer me even a semblance of privacy. I turned toward Hinton Park, remembering that before the entrance there was a path that led to a small center with pictures and descriptions of the wildlife along with maps of the trails. No one would be in there on a cold Sunday morning. Or at least I prayed no one would be.

A relieved exhale left me as I pushed open the door and noticed the empty interior. I had never been in the building, having never really been interested in learning about the wildlife of the area. A squirrel was just a squirrel as far as I was concerned. One tree was no different than another. I didn't care how many miles I would get in taking one trail or another. But the inside of this center was peaceful.

Every footstep echoed off the walls as I walked over to a wooden bench. A name was burnt into the wood, a donation to the park in memory of one of the residents of the area. My fingers ran over the name, forcing me to think of my own mortality. Life was too short.

I sat down and turned on the screen of my phone. My finger hovered over the message application, wondering if I should read his messages before committing to calling him. Did I really want to know what he had to say? Did it really matter? Was it going to change how I felt? I debated back and forth, my own brain playing Devil's advocate for every reason why reading beforehand would better prepare me for our conversation. But if I thought too hard about what I wanted to say in the moment, when that time actually came, I'd be left with nothing. I questioned whether my words would form anyways, my nerves drying out my throat and producing a lump in my stomach from just thinking about it. Unintentionally, my finger brushed the screen and opened his messages. My eyes, completely intentionally, read every word at lightning speed. I went all the way back to the first time stamp of a missed message.

Where you at? You coming back?
Are you okay? Where'd you go?
What happened?
Are you okay?
Did something happen?
Are you angry? Can we talk?
Whatever happened, I'm sorry. Can we talk?
Are you there?

Over and over, message upon message begging me to reach out. Tears formed in my eyes. Was he so oblivious? Did he really think I wouldn't notice? Or did he really not understand what happened? Was he concerned about me or just that he got caught? Every question to flood me was another excuse not to give in. Maybe this was another instance where my sister would tell me to just run.

After a certain time, Chase stopped messaging and started trying to call every thirty minutes or so. I bit my lip as I stared at my phone. The clock mocked me, forcing me to acknowledge that every second I didn't act was another second of this torture. A digit changed as a minute passed and I took a deep breath. Now or never, I guess.

I closed my eyes as my finger hovered over the phone icon. It was never going to get easier. My finger pressed down on my screen. My eyes opened to notice I clicked on the wrong thing, almost sending a smiley face impression to one of his messages of concern. I panicked and quickly clicked away, hitting the phone icon in the process. My heart accelerated, not having meant to force myself into the moment directly after almost screwing everything up.

The first dial tone barely finished before his voice came through.

"Hello, Alex? Is that you? I've been trying to call, but you probs know that. Are you okay? What happened?"

Words threatened to pour out of me like a flood, the dams finding release. I glanced about, ensuring I didn't miss seeing anyone who may be able to hear. I wasn't going to let him act dumb. I wasn't going to let him play me. Not again.

"What happened?" I asked, anger filling my tone, which threatened to crack as my nerves escalated. "And you didn't just show the whole world that you still have feelings for Sara? What am I? Seriously. What did you want from me? What do you still want from me? Don't use me in some fucked up game of 5D chess. I'm a person, one who had actual feelings for you."

"What are you talking about?"

"Let me clue you in if you're really so dumb not to get it. Most guys don't just let their exes massage their backs and whisper sweet words into their ears while the one they invited is left to the smelly, filthy inside just to watch it all unfold. You really think I wouldn't feel hurt. That it was all so reasonable to you."

"Oh." Chase released a nervous chuckle. He fumbled over finding a word to start.

"It's really not funny," I clapped back, tears filling my eyes as I felt belittled. Bullied. I hadn't been betrayed, that would have required him actually caring in the first place. Yet rather than blaze him with every curse I could think, my mind kept reverting to the same self-deprecating things. It's not his fault I'm so stupid that I didn't see it coming from a mile away.

"I just, I think I understand now." His breathing grew shallow, and he murmured into the phone. "I'm such a fucking idiot."

Silence fell between us for a moment, enough time to dive into my purse and pull out the extra napkins I swiped up at the food court. Tears streamed in controlled rivers down my face. I sniffled, capturing any mucus that escaped me. Pressure fell from my shoulders with every heave of my chest, as if the hyperventilating from my sobs actually helped relieve me.

"Alex, I know I'm stupid for saying this. But it really wasn't what it looked like. I don't know what you saw, but I promise, it wasn't what you're thinking."

I bit my lip, maintaining my silence. Defending myself and my thoughts, validating my feelings and my reaction, it wasn't worth it. He would need to explain himself. He would have to use his energy to fix this if that's what he wanted. I had made up my mind. This was no longer my burden to mend.

"I was helping Dean. You know that. She came over when Roger went inside to bring some tools and I was stuck holding that stupid thing. I couldn't move. I was stuck. She just started doing, well, what she does. I told her to stop, I did. It was all super uncomfortable. Dean tried to tell her too, ask him, he'll tell you what went down. It's just, uhh, I'm such an idiot."

I turned the phone on speaker and set it down on the bench next to me. I curled into my stomach, embracing myself, squeezing my eyes shut. His words went in and out as I had to filter away the pain. He stumbled, he stuttered. His words felt hollow and dense at the same time. The crack in his voice pleaded, yet the words he spoke mocked me.

"Can we just talk? Please. Face to face. I don't want to do it like this."

His tone begged for an answer. He begged to be heard, to be seen. But he knew. He knew that I was so attracted to him I was willing to ignore that he was still in a relationship the first time we ate out. He knew that with the tiniest bit of affection I would leave behind my doubts of the words he spoke. He knew his presence was my weakness. He couldn't defend himself without his gestures and gentle caresses being the default to convince me that everything was okay. To convince me that he cared.

With a deep breath, I sat up. My hands rubbed against my face as I tried to rid my cheeks of the red coloring, as I tried to squash the bags that were already formed beneath my eyes. I picked up my phone and turned the speaker off.

"I don't think there's anything left to be said."

"What?"

The word left from his lips so quickly. They barely contained a tone, leaving like a single note of a piano. I choked back another stream of tears and continued.

"You don't realize how betrayed I feel? How insecure this all made me? I already didn't feel worthy of your touch, of your affection. I'm done with these games." My words fought to find strength, but they were left reaching. "I'm not like her. I'm nothing like her. I don't need the drama. I don't need the excitement of losing you only to have you plead with me."

"I never expected you to be like her."

"I may have just lost my best friend because of all of this. You think I'm worried about fixing this? About finding common ground with you just to have it happen time and time again? We're both stupid if we ever thought this was going to work."

"You can't mean that."

"My best friend, who has been loyal to me since day one. And it's all my fault. It's my fault that I ever trusted in someone like you."

"Someone... like me?"

I licked my lips, wondering the intention with which he heard my words. I figured it was understood differently than I meant, but I couldn't care to defend myself. I couldn't care to retract what I said.

"I just... I need time, Chase. I need time."

A prolonged silence almost left me wondering if he was even listening anymore. Maybe he had walked away from the phone in anger, in frustration. An audible breath came across and I closed my eyes. It was amazing how in such times a breath could mean a million things.

"There's nothing I could do that would make you want to talk this out?"

"No, I don't think so."

Another clearly audible breath.

"Well, we'll catch up later then, I guess. Take care, Alex. I just want you to know that I'm sorry."

Before I even had the time to respond, he hung up. A weight lifted off my shoulders as a new one settled in. As I pressed to leave the call, the ever-growing urge of wanting to chuck my phone across the room itched at my fingertips. I quickly hid it in my purse, not wanting any further regrets to build up as my emotions ate away at me.

I stared at the ground. The desire to cry built as a pressure formed in my chest, expanding like a balloon being blown up, threatening to pop at any second. A scream formed in my throat, begging for release.

But as my mouth opened, as I agreed to drop the flood gates once more to let my tears flow, I was left with nothing. No sound came. No tears formed. Emotionally and mentally, I had exhausted myself. Between the night before through today, I used up every last bit of energy I had to cry, to feel bad for myself. Now I was just tired. My body felt heavy and numb. My face felt stiff and lumpy. I felt everything and I felt nothing. I just wanted to sleep and hope that when I woke up, I'd realize that everything had gone back to the way it was several weeks ago.

Of all the places I could go next, my bed being the first, I couldn't help but think about Jordyn. She hated me, of that I was sure. I would need to find a way to get to her. To let her know how stupid and sorry I was.

I withdrew my phone from my purse and scrolled through our messages. Some of the older ones brought smiles to my face as I remembered the events that came before or those that would follow. So many happy memories... They felt distant.

"How am I supposed to fix this?" I mumbled, reading message after message in hopes of some clue that would pop out at me. "It's like mountain climbing without a harness. I'll either reach the top and everything will be okay. Or I'll fall to my death, no one ever being able to recover my body. And with my great decision-making skills, the latter seems the most likely." I sighed.

My eyes stopped on a message about her new favorite band playing at the Lounge. She always goes up there. If she wouldn't answer a knock on her door, then I'd have to find her in the wild, a.k.a. a place where she couldn't simply avoid me.

"But I can't just walk up to her, she'll punch me out. There's got to be another way."

My eyes focused on my screen, hoping the answer would jump out and find me. A conversation of voices made me flinch as an elderly couple entered the little lodge. I stood from the memorial bench and acted as though I was looking around, hoping they wouldn't notice the dismal state of my face.

A chunk of smoothed stone caught my eye. It sat to the side of the bench and contained a quote in remembrance of the woman whose name was engraved there.

"Life is a balance of love and failures. You must fail to appreciate the good. You must love to know why you rise from the fall."

Chapter Nineteen

The crowd at the Lounge was a bit larger than I expected. It helped me to blend in a bit, but I also struggled to find her among the masses. I stood at the bar on my tiptoes, searching over the many heads for her.

"She's coming up here now," the bartender warned me.

I hid my face behind a blanket of hair I let fall in front of me.

"What can I get for you?" the bartender asked.

"I'll take any fruity juice you got in ginger ale." Jordyn's voice answered, lacking its usual energy.

I bit my lip and tried to catch a glance of her face, but I didn't want to risk being seen. After everything I had done the past week, the worst thing to happen would be her walking out now. I needed everything to go according to plan, and her being here was enough to tell me that at least I'd get a shot.

Once she got her drink and turned away, I flipped my hair back. Doing so felt so amazing since I chopped the pink ends off, my hair looking healthier than it had in years. I had also treated myself to a new brand of facial scrub, the smell of apricots on my skin always calming me. When you've got no one but you, self-care is critical to get right. Between the pampering and studying, I still managed to find time to put this plan together. Maybe my time management skills were improving.

The MC came on stage, and I almost jumped from my seat as excitement and nerves started to settle in.

"Up next, we got the next hot thing to hit this campus. They've played here before and they got a special set list tonight. Put your hands together for We Hunt the Monsters!"

The crowd cheered. I stood from my seat and yelled and hooted for the band. I raised my hands over my head, applauding as they entered. As I sat back down, the bartender and I shared a smile, his was amused, mine demonstrated my nerves.

"Hello, everyone. We have a special show for you tonight. We also got a new song to share," James, the lead singer of the group addressed the crowd. His words were mumbled into the microphone pressing against his lips. "Hope you enjoy."

The crowd cheered again. Jordyn jumped up and down, no longer able to contain her excitement as she stood near the edge of the stage. A grin found its way to my face, happy that she could find happiness with herself and the things she enjoyed.

Song after song played. The pressure on my shoulders grew less and less, even though I knew the time would come. I found myself relaxing, the bartender and I talking back and forth about some of the most random things. Everything felt like it was falling into place. For the first time in a few weeks, I felt liberated of every anxiety that forced me to act a certain way to appease others. Maybe it had been more than weeks of that performance. I think back to my mom and all of her ex-boyfriends and ex-husbands. I had been putting on a performance my entire life. This past week, I felt none of that pressure. In my loneliness, I finally realized I had me all along.

"Next up is a special song," James muttered into the mic. "We haven't practiced it too many times, but we wanted to share it with you all in our first performance of it here tonight. It was written with the help of a good friend. Hope you enjoy."

The bartender slid an orange soda to me as the opening notes filled the air. I bit down on my lip, the butterflies taking flight in my stomach. This was it.

Paper wings to the fire
Cliff jumping to my funeral pyre
Erase my name, it's all the same

My headstone needs no identifier
Or maybe just ashes
Thrown into the air
No mercy from the breeze or wind
Won't support my sin
Refuse to be the ones that take me there

I'm just looking for retribution
From this botched self-execution
Don't deserve your thoughts
Don't deserve your prayers
Just want my words to reach your ears

I'm sorry, I apologize
I was so wrong and I realize it was never worth a guy
I beg you to hear me
To see into my eyes
I don't need forgiveness
Just want to grieve less
Knowing you'll be alright

So Jordyn, I'm sorry
I apologize
I was so stupid and wrong
So I wrote you this song
In hopes that you'll see the sadness in my eyes

Jordyn, I'm sorry
I beg you to hear it one last time
Don't deserve forgiveness
Just hope you know this
I'll never find another like you in my life

But even I know that you'll be alright
I apologize

THE CROWD ERUPTED AS the last notes of the song blasted through the club. Rather than dance or jump up and down, Jordyn had backed up to her seat during the course of the song, her head swiveling to try to find me, or so I assumed.

I downed the glass of soda and slid my tab and tip to the bartender. He winked at me, and I snuck out the door before the next song started. Tears formed in my eyes as a smile found its way through. My stomach swirled to the odd concoction of emotion. Sadness, despair, happiness, joy, peace. They all found me.

I rounded the Lounge to the back entrance where the bands enter and sat in the back of their pickup truck. The door opening to the bed of the trunk was unmistakable, covered in all kinds of bumper stickers and a huge logo of their band. I wrapped my coat about myself more tightly, trying to conserve my warmth in the chill of the cold night. To distract myself, not wanting to think about what just happened too hard, I scrolled through my phone to see if the exam scores for the week had come through yet. I noticed I aced them all, my overall grades in the class improving with the score. I sighed in relief.

As my fingers grew numb in the cold, the screech of the metal door caused me to jump. I leapt down from the truck and rushed over to the group. Without thinking, my arms wrapped about James.

"That was so great," I said, taking in the warmth of his arms embracing me in return. I backed away and rummaged through my purse. "Here's the other half. Thank you, guys, so much for everything."

"No, thank you," James said. The other three members nodded and agreed with their front man. "It was fun working with you this past week. I'm just happy we could make it work."

"Yeah, I just hope she heard it."

"Oh, I did."

Her voice alone caused a skip in my heart. I turned to see Jordyn standing in the shadow the building, staring at the bunch of us. A moment of silence passed between us, neither knowing what to say. Jordyn took a couple of steps before it transformed into a full on sprint and tackle to embrace me. My arms constricted her, as if not applying enough pressure would ensure she'd get away again.

"I'm so sorry," I muttered over and over again, tears sliding down my cheeks. When we finally parted, I continued. "I'm so stupid. I am literally the worst friend ever to miss your big night. You had every right to be mad at me. I was mad at me. I didn't know if I could fix it, but I just wanted you to hear me and know that. I'm sorry."

My rambling almost came through as incoherent, even to me. Words were not my strong suit in times when it really mattered to get it right. When she didn't respond right away, I assumed the worst. But after a moment, a passing car's headlights hit her face at just the right angle to notice her face covered in streams of tears. I wrapped my arms about her again.

"Whatever happens next, just know that you were the best friend anyone could ever ask for," I whispered into her ears.

"I hate you so much," Jordyn mumbled, her voice cracking as she sniffled the mucus away. "But I love you so much too. That makes me hate you even more."

We both laughed. I realized that I'd broken through. I'd get another chance.

The guys from the band huddled about us and consumed us in a group hug. I giggled as I noticed Jordyn almost swoon at their touch. As we formed a circle, James's arm landed across my shoulders, two of the other members each taking one of Jordyn's arms in theirs.

"We normally hit this awesome buffet down the street after our gigs. You ladies want to join us?"

Jordyn answered before I even had the chance to consider the question. Her acceptance was mine. Wherever she went, I wanted to follow.

"Awesome. Let's go."

We walked down the sidewalk as a group. I felt a bit on edge, thinking that the other passerby might think our large group suspicious. But all they had to do was listen to Jordyn gushing over the guys for two seconds to realize it was just a band with their groupies. My paranoia left as soon as it came, a new sensation flooding over me as I could feel the heat of him peering at me out of the corner of his eyes.

"I know I've said it more than a million times this week, but I think what you did for your friend was super cool." James spoke in a way that was so casual for one with countless fans in the local area and across the internet. His compliment made me giggle in thanks, as if his notice of what I did made all the difference. "And hey, anytime you get another idea for a song, hit us up. I'd love to work with you again."

"I'll definitely do that," I laughed, brushing some stray hairs from my face. "But I don't think I have any other songs in me. I'm just a one hit wonder, I guess."

He laughed and placed his arm across my shoulders again, pulling me in a bit closer.

"I doubt that," he whispered under his breath.

A breeze hit me as a small group ran by. Dean spun in a circle as he jogged past, his eyes meeting mine. They quickly found one of his other buddies. My heart sank. I recognized the hoodie and the form. But he refused to turn around, to look at me. No doubt he had already seen me. He had already seen the way James drew me in. A headache started to form as a mountain of worries and nerves erupted through every other thought of the evening. Despite all that had happened that past week, he continued to be a fleeting thought, always returning for me to shoo away time and time again. But nonetheless returning.

James opened the door to the buffet and let me through before passing the opened door to a friend so he could follow in behind me. He led the group to a table where we talked for a bit before getting our food. Jordyn laughed and joked, sitting across from me, between two members of the band, flirting with them both in hopes of snatching at least one for another date. And I assumed if it came down to it, she would be up for an open relationship with them both, which didn't seem too far out of the picture.

Despite listening and laughing at their anecdotes as a band, between their practices, their signings, and their concerts, my mind couldn't help but wander. I kept glancing out the windows, wondering if he would pass by again. The soccer team had some big games coming up as the end of the season approached. I had been scoping out the schedule earlier in the week. Though I wouldn't be able to travel for their game tomorrow, it didn't keep me from crossing my fingers and wishing any higher power above for their victory.

The tug of war occurring inside my mind kept him there. I couldn't decide whether to end it all together, or at least try to maintain a friendship. I wanted to see him succeed. I wanted to see him happy. But would happiness ever find either of us or would we continually cling to the memories of the past? Would we never be able to see past what happened and move on to what could be?

I stirred about the lo mein on my plate, unaware if I could eat anymore. As his mates went on about some moment they found hilarious, James found the courage to place a hand on my thigh. I flinched.

"Sorry," he whispered, red rushing to his cheeks as if embarrassed.

"It's... There's someone else."

My eyes avoided his and focused on my plate. Out of my peripheral vision, I could see him bite his lip and furrow his brow at the empty plate in front of him.

"After everything... I didn't realize."

"It's my fault. I didn't think it was even worth mentioning."

He snorted a laugh.

"Not exactly the kind of thing you don't mention."

"You're right." I could tell my comment caught him off guard as he turned to face me in an instant. My eyes met his. "I tried not to mention him, talk about in any way, even think about him. I tried but I think I've realized that it's not so easy to just forget about someone you care about."

Our table went silent as the three other members stood to grab their next plate. Jordyn sat there and stared across the table at us. I released an anxious breath and shook my head.

"Maybe I'm stupid, actually I know I am. But I can't help but think that there's hope now. This is my chance to start over and do things the right way. I refuse to mess up this time."

Chapter Twenty

"And who was in power in Persia when the Battle of Marathon occurred," I asked, checking my notes just to make sure the answer in my head was the correct one.

"King Darius the first," Jordyn responded, flicking a piece of popcorn into the air and trying to catch it in her mouth. She missed for the fifth time.

"Correct. What were the most powerful cities in Phoenicia?"

"Umm... Tyre and Sicily?"

"Try again."

"Umm... Oh, Tyre and Sidon!"

"Yep, that's what we're looking for."

I flipped to the next page in my notes and laughed at the doodle I made of wildflowers in a soccer field. It felt like so long ago that I had drawn it.

"What is it? Let me see."

"It's-" She grabbed the notebook from my hand, grinning at the image with no amusement on her face. "It's nothing."

"Man, you really fell head over heels for him in such a short time. Got too many hormones stocked up or what?"

I rubbed my head and swiped my notebook back from her, closing it in hopes that even if she did grab it back, she'd never find the page. Biting the inside of my lip, I chose not to respond to her question and instead flipped through the pages of my ancient civilizations book opened on her dorm room floor.

"Has he reached out to you lately? Have you asked him about his fuck up and if he's willing to change?"

"We talked very shortly the day after. I just... I wasn't willing to give him the time of day to talk to him in person. I didn't have the energy."

"Yeah, but you told me that he seemed oblivious, like it didn't even mean anything to him so it shouldn't to you either. If he really thinks like that, is that someone you want to keep fawning after?"

"Maybe you're right."

I glanced up from the floor and scanned all of the art on her wall, her newest poster of We Hunt the Monsters blocking out some of the other bands she followed in the past. The corner of my mouth twisted up.

"But, even if you are right, I still haven't convinced my brain that I'm ready to just move on."

I sighed and threw myself to the ground to stare at the ceiling. She pushed our books away and joined me there. Without hesitation, she offered me the piece of popcorn in her hand. I laughed.

"Is that not the one you just fished from under your bed because you missed your mouth?"

"And?"

"And you expect me to eat it lying down and not somehow choke and die from it getting stuck in my throat."

"Well, now you're just being dramatic, aren't you."

We laughed and collectively sighed.

Thoughts of ancient civilizations filled my head. I imagined how they had so much more to worry about than some petty boy drama. They were scared of wars, or soldiers coming to their towns to burn their houses, entire cities razed to the ground. They worried about their next meals in times of drought. They scraped by with the minimal of necessities to provide for their families. And yet here I was, lying on the floor of my friend's heated dorm room, scared and anxious of talking and possibly obsessing again over the same guy who had been in my dreams for weeks now.

"Oh, hey." Jordyn sat up and reached across her bed. She pulled out a scrap of paper from under her pillow. "They're doing that poetry readings opened up to the public again. I already started on my next one. I just have one week to get it done though."

"That's so awesome. Uhh, I'm so angry and frustrated I didn't make it to your first reading."

"You were drowning in your sorrows. I already told you I forgive you."

"I know, but it doesn't make me feel any less shitty."

"Well, then don't miss this next one." Her alarm sounded. "Ooh. Our takeout is here. Gotta run down."

"Wait," I growled and reached into my purse to throw my wallet at her. "I'm paying."

"Ouch. You think I'm some sportsball player?" She rubbed her arm where my wallet hit and ran out of the room.

I giggled as the door shut behind her. With the loudest sigh I could conjure, I let it go. Relief washed over me. Of all that could have happened, in every way in which things could have gone wrong, they didn't.

I stretched my arms and folded them behind my head.

"My sister was right," I mumbled, almost not believing the words to come out of my mouth. "Just had to find the right language."

My eyes moved to my ancient civilization's notebook, imagining the doodle of the soccer ball in a wildflower field. I allowed my eyelids to block my vision and fell into the land of daydreaming.

With a full stomach and head full of We Hunt the Monsters songs that Jordyn decided to blast after getting a string of ten questions right, I searched for my keys in my pocket to open the door. As I entered, Sara turned around, bobby pin in mouth and hands twisting her hair above her head, mirror leaning against the wall in front of her. Seeing my face, she returned to what she was doing.

I set my backpack on the floor and jumped into my bed to scroll through my phone. As I hit the comforter, a sharp pain jabbed me in the side.

"Ow!"

"Oh, right," Sara said, removing the bobby pin from her mouth and positioning it just right in her hair. "Casey brought that package. Said it wouldn't fit in your mail bin at the office, so she just brought it up. Doesn't say who it's from, I checked."

"Thanks for checking."

I rolled my eyes and observed the package. It was quite large, and I couldn't remember ordering anything. My name was on the shipping address, and I didn't recognize the sender's address. I reached across my desk for a pair of scissors and sliced through the tape, a layer on top of an already broken layer. My eyes scanned Sara, wondering if she tried to hide already having opened it as well. Pulling the flaps back, a smile sprang to life on my face.

Inside the box were art supplies: Charcoal pencils, markers of supreme quality, an entire spectrum of sketch pencils, a set of basic watercolors, brushes in several sizes, and a drawing pad for mixed media. On top of the supplies lay an envelope. I opened it up and found two pieces of paper. One was a folded-up page from the drawing pads, the other a torn-out page from a notebook.

Hey Alex,

I had already ordered this before, well, you know. Didn't want it to go to waste so figured I'd just send it to you like this. Hope you like it. I did test out everything just to make sure they worked. I'm no artist though so don't judge too harshly.

Chase

I giggled at the note, holding it in my hands and staring at it. I read it time and time and time again, hearing his voice recite the words, a breathy laugh coming through as I tried to understand what he meant by the last line. I looked to the folded-up paper that came in the envelope.

As I pulled back the corner, a beautiful array of colors hit me, and my heart skipped a beat. It was us. He drew us, sitting in a field. There was a soccer ball at our feet. I had a drawing pad on my lap. He looked up to the clouds. We held hands. We looked so peaceful, so happy. I questioned whether he drew this before or after the party. And yet, the question left as soon as it came. I honestly did not care.

I hugged the drawing tight to me, never wanting to let it go. The longer I thought about it, the happier it made me. He found my language. He found the way to reach me. He did care.

The alarm sounded on my phone, pulling me from my daze. I refolded the drawing along the same lines he had folded them, and I put it in my sweatshirt pocket. I silenced the alarm, grabbed the bottled orange soda that remained from my time with Jordyn, and ran to the student lounge below.

My fingers moved at lightning speed to find the stream. The national anthem was being sung as the soccer players took to the field. My heart fluttered as I saw him in the lineup. My fists clenched, so excited to watch him play, hoping the coach would give him time in this game. I crossed my fingers and bit my lip as the first kick off occurred. Though I failed to understand the calls and all the sportscasters were saying, I did understand one thing. The way to win was to get the ball in the net of the opposing team. And the way to do that was to be better, in every way, than your opponent.

Chase didn't start, but every time the cameras showed the sidelines, I waved at him. He cheered for his team, pacing back and forth as he watched the ball. Every so often, he would jump up and down, not wanting his muscles to go cold. I clapped my hands then clasped my fingers together, praying to whatever higher power may be listening that he would be allowed his chance.

After half time, my prayers were answered. He took to the field. I no longer cared to watch the ball and whoever was in possession of it. I only had eyes for him. Every time he got to kick, pass, or defend, I sat on the edge of my seat. Any others in the lounge probably thought I was crazy. And I felt that way myself. I couldn't contain my joy, my excitement. I wanted to throw my phone when the refs would pull a yellow card on our team. And despite all their sweat, all their tears and hard work, the team wouldn't see victory.

I closed the tab as the stream ended and sighed as I stared out the window. I wanted to text him, tell him I watched the whole thing. But he probably had a long bus ride back. I didn't want to bother him. He was with his teammates, and he probably just wanted to vent his frustrations with them then rest on the way back.

Putting down my phone, I couldn't wait for Sunday to come, which is not something I would have imagined saying a week ago. I was on a streak of luck, hard fought for and hard-won luck. I didn't want that streak to end now.

Wrapping my arms across my stomach, I squeezed tight, hearing the paper bend ever so slightly as I embraced every little thing that it meant to me.

Chapter Twenty-One

When Sunday morning came, I jumped out of bed, not even needing my alarm to wake me, and headed straight to the bathrooms for my ritual morning facial scrub. My heart raced as excitement filled me. With a joyous hop to my jog, I descended the stairs and ran straight for the food court. The peace and tranquility of a weekend morning used to seem haunting. Now, it was my favorite time of the week. No crowds, no ruckus, no worries.

After ordering my usual breakfast, I sat at one of the cleanest tables around and pulled out my chemistry homework. Question after question, the answers flowed from me. Flipping back and forth to my periodic table print out, I was able to get through every equation by the time I stuffed the last bit of sandwich down my throat. I hoped it was a demonstration of how my luck would be going that day.

With no shame to be found, I withdrew my drawing pad and some graphite pencils of the desired gradient and began sketching an image. I wanted to transpose the doodle from my ancient civilization's notebook on to a larger scale. Not to mention I wanted it to look better, taking my time to be meticulous about the details. From the shading to the proportions, the image needed to be more than just pencil on paper. I wanted this picture to speak one million and one words just by looking at it. The memories, the laughter, the affection. I wanted it all to come through.

As noon approached, my fingers fidgeted, checking his online status as frequently as I possibly could. I wanted the moment to be perfect. A text from Jordyn came through.

You busy? Want to get together?

I bit my lip and thought carefully through my words.

Maybe later. I'm hoping to meet up with Chase

You go get it. Make him an offer he can't refuse!

I giggled. Checking his status again, I saw nothing had changed. I sighed.

"Now or never, I guess."

I opened the chat log and initiated what I hoped would be the start of something new.

Hey, can we talk?

I stared at the words I've typed, reading them time and time again, before pressing send. My stomach swirled as anxiety filled me.

"The worst that could happen is he says no, and I move on. Yeah. If he's no longer interested, I would just move on."

After a few shallow breaths, I realized how hard that would hit me. To just move on, let go and pretend like none of it ever happened, I would probably break down again until I could relieve myself of the sadness. So many memories that sprung to my head from the simplest of tasks. So many things that reminded me of him. It almost wouldn't seem fair that so many things would be ruined should that be the outcome. Then again, maybe it wasn't fair that I made him wait.

No one wants to be told they have to wait for someone else to be ready. He may have already found someone else. He may have already moved on. With his looks and talent, I had no doubt that wouldn't be a problem for him.

I refined the lines of the blades of grass sticking up from under the soccer ball, casting their shadow where it made the most sense given the light's origin for the piece. The side of my hand was covered in graphite smears as I moved from one area to the next with little care how I dragged my hand across the paper. I almost didn't mind, as it created a softness to the lines that I could probably never achieve intentionally. My phone vibrated, causing me to throw my pencil down and turn on the screen.

I'm at the gym right now. Maybe later

Having a location was good enough for me. I packed up my supplies and hopped, skipped, and sprinted for the door. My lungs screamed as the brisk winter air filled them. Every breath more painful than the last. But not even the hurt could deter me. My sides started to cramp.

"Damn, I really should have stretched first..."

My backpack rattled behind me as I went. The sounds of pencils shimmying out of their case and my books in turn crushing them made me gasp. After checking, I realized it was a false alarm, but with that brief stop I wondered if I could get myself back up to speed.

"What if he was already cleaning up? What if he already left? I'm exerting all this energy to possibly not even see him?"

That was enough to rev my engines and get me running like a horde of zombies chased after me. Or even worse, my mother with some more "great" relationship advice. I shook my head.

"Yeah, not doing that again."

When I made it to the gym, I laughed at the thought that I had already had a sufficient workout. I flashed my student ID at the desk and wandered the corridor, peaking through the different rooms in search of Chase.

At long last I found him at the indoor field, setting up his soccer ball for a kick angled away from the net, trying to maneuver his foot just right to get a goal. The first kick I saw, he missed. I scrunched my nose, hoping it wasn't a sign that he was having a bad day. He mumbled to himself, eyes focused solely on the ball and the net.

I followed the wall to where he was and set my backpack and coat down. He still hadn't noticed me, committed to making the shot. I crossed my fingers, hoping this would be the one. His head moved from the ball to the goal, making slight adjustments to his stance. He swung his leg back and his foot hooked around the ball, it bounced from the post and straight for me.

My hands flew up to shield myself, blocking my vision, only to have the ball fly straight past me. I exhaled in relief. When I brought my head up, he stared at me.

"Alex? What are you doing here?"

"Well, you told me this is where you were. And I wanted to be where you were."

He furrowed his brow, not in anger but in confusion, and sprinted to where his soccer ball rolled. As he jogged back, his eyes never left mine. He stopped in front of me.

"I told you we would talk later. I'm practicing right now."

"And you can practice away. I just wanted to watch."

His eyes widened and he shook his head as a breathy chuckle forced its way through.

"What? You want to watch so you can make fun of how much I suck?"

"I want to watch because seeing you through the screen of my phone playing on the field just wasn't enough to satisfy me. I want to see the real thing."

Chase's smile dropped and he looked away. He brought up his hand to scratch his neck as he eyed the net on the field.

"That's embarrassing. Of all the games you could have watched, you watched the one where I barely got any time at all. Not to mention those misses."

"I thought you guys played great. Especially you."

A smile formed on my face, eyes inviting him to join me. Yet no matter how I attempted the flirty, overly happy to see him expression, his own refused to mirror mine.

"Alex," he said, dragging out my name as if it hurt him to say. My smile vanished. "You said you needed your time, well now I need mine."

His words hit like a freight train. My jaw dropped, but I couldn't respond. There were no words left in me to respond to that. Silence fell between us for the moment, enough weight to crush us both.

"If you want to just move on, why can't you just tell me?" I pressed in a whisper. His eyes found mine with a glare I didn't understand.

"Move on? I'm not the one already seeing other people. I thought you needed time to settle some emotions, fix your friendship. Turns out you were just trying with other guys. You bash me and Sara, but that's over, we're through. We had our chance, and I didn't want that anymore."

"It's not what you think-"

"It never is though, right? It's always just me or you or someone not understanding."

My heart raced enough for me to think it a medical emergency. I felt like my entire body was shutting down. How could everything else have gone so right for this to have gone so wrong? Was that the balance? My lungs that burned before now gasped for air. It was time for fight or flight, and I wanted an escape. But after everything I'd been through, I didn't want to give up. Our emotions and hormones were raging. How could I ever get through to him my intention? I needed my words to reach him. I needed to find a language he would understand.

I grabbed the ball from his hands and sprinted to the field.

"Alex!"

Irritation laced his voice as he followed me to where I stood. I placed the ball several feet from the goal and eyed it a couple of times despite not really understanding why.

"What are you doing? I'm not the only one trying to practice, you know."

"Just give me one sec."

I jogged to the net and spread my arms out wide.

"If I block your kick, you have to give me a chance to talk to you. Just a couple of minutes. But, if you get the ball past me, then you get to choose what happens next. If that-"

"You're gonna get hurt."

"If that means you never want to see my face again, I'll respect that and do my best to make it happen. But you have to make it past me."

Chase bit his lip as a thin grin formed, despite his desire to suppress it. His shoulders moved up and down as he fought back his laughter. I took a deep breath, almost afraid of what would happen if he did actually decide to kick it. If it came for me, my best bet was really to dodge out of the way. No doubt his kicks would leave me looking bruised and battered. But I had to try. I needed my chance.

He rolled the ball around with the tip of his toes. Dribbling it from foot to foot, he drew nearer the net.

"Woah, woah, not too close. I'm already at a disadvantage."

"Maybe it might be easier to just steal the ball from me then."

He kicked the ball a few inches away and walked forward to it, tempting me to do as he suggested. I lowered my stance and prepared for the inevitable kick. But it never came.

Chase stopped a few inches from me and placed the ball under his foot.

"Well? You can come get it now or it will be past you by the time you even try to react."

"You're actually gonna give me the chance to steal it?"

"It's the only way you'll win this bet."

I licked my lips and watched the ball. He stood on it, no muscle in his body bouncing as if to betray his words. I rose from my sumo stance and took a step toward him. I stared straight forward at his chin and took a breath.

As fast as I could move my leg, I swung at the ball. Before I realized, he had already passed to the other foot. I turned to see the soccer ball roll slowly into the net. As it hit the netting, I questioned what the point of this even was. I closed my eyes and sighed.

"Well, you won. So, what is it? Do you just need time? Or do you really never want to see me again?"

A gentle pressure landed on my waist. My eyes rose to meet his but before they could do so, I was met with his lips. It lasted no more than a second, but it was enough of an answer to flood me with relief and joy.

"Give me a sec to grab my things and wash up a bit," Chase said, brushing a strand of hair from my face. I nodded; no other words able to form in response.

He jogged for his soccer ball then grabbed a water bottle and wraps at the side of the net before taking off for the locker room. I leaned my back against the gym wall and looked to the ceiling, a cheesy smile spread across my face. Suppressing a squeal of excitement, I tossed my bag over my shoulder and made for the front lobby.

I sent him a text when I got there, biting my lip as I admired the picture next to his name. Doubt and hesitation tried to erase my happiness as every fond memory poured over me. Perhaps it was a bit dramatic, a week worth of memories could really mean just how much... But it was more than enough that I'd be getting another chance to expand upon those moments.

Hands landed on my shoulders and massaged them with a tender affection. My head leaned back to gaze upon his beautifully sculpted face. The lights of the lobby dazzled in his eyes, his smile so bright I almost thought he may be just as relieved as I was.

After a moment of staring into the other's eyes, he moved to take a seat next to me and wrapped an arm about my shoulders. He pulled me in for a kiss on the cheek.

"So, you wanted to talk?" he asked, a smirk crossing his face as his eyes looked me up and down.

I pressed down on my coat in my lap, squeezing the fabric between my fingers. Nerves filled me, my stomach tossing and turning at the thought of screwing it all up now.

"Umm. I just wanted to say that, umm. Thank you for the art supplies."

"So, you're just here to thank me? Could have just sent a card."

"That picture you drew." His face softened. "It was beautiful. It made me feel warm and happy and..." The saliva was building up in my mouth. My words grew jumbled in my head and I tried my best to sort through them. "When I saw it, I just wanted to be with you. By you. Near you. Whatever.

"I tuned into the game. Well, I was going to anyways, but this made me want to do so even more. I saw you and..." My eyes connected with his, melting into his deep brown irises. They followed a steady path to his lips then down his neck. He hadn't yet put on a jacket, his t-shirt pressing against him making me wish I was able to do the same. I could already feel the eyes observing us, nobody ever able to mind their own business it seemed. I gulped and the words poured out all at once.

"Every time I see you, I just think about how wrong everything went so fast. I think we tried to rush it too close to your breakup. I wasn't mentally ready. You weren't emotionally prepared. All kinds of boundaries were crossed. But then I see you, and none of that matters. I just want to be in your arms. With you, near you. Everything I touch, everything I do, everywhere I go, I'm reminded of you. I just-"

"Same," he interrupted, his frown expressing the hurt he must have been sharing with me.

I stopped to catch my breath. With that one word, every doubt paralyzing my muscles, every fear swirling in my stomach, every pressure constricting my mind vanished. My hand landed on his thigh, my fingers sliding together slightly experiencing the soft texture of his sweatpants. He flinched as if my movements tickled him, but quickly placed a hand over mine so I wouldn't move it away. The pressure and warmth of his palm on the back of my hand sent a flurry of heat through me. My cheeks flushed.

"It's silly to say now," I started, my eyes watching our hands, "but I always wished you and Sara would never break up. I didn't want you to stop coming to our room. I wanted to see you. Sure, I hated being there when a group of you guys would come over for drinks and games, but I forced myself to stay just to see you."

I giggled and his hand tightened about mine. My eyes found him.

"Sometimes I felt I just stayed with her so I could see you more often." Chase snickered and shook his head. "Almost crazy how fast my heart got when that bottle landed on me. Felt like I had just played a hundred minutes straight on the field."

"Seriously? But you were so calm about the whole thing. I thought I was going to puke with all the nerves. I was so shocked you actually went through with it."

My eyes glazed over as I now stared past him, picturing the day like it was yesterday. Remembering my shock as we squeezed into the closet, my heart fighting to escape as his skin brushed against mine. The heat from his breath. The taste on his lips. Time must have stopped because it seemed to last forever and yet not long enough at the same time.

"I would have hated myself if I decided Sara's word was mine. Especially knowing what I know now."

His hand lifted from mine and fell upon my cheek.

"I would love the chance to get to know you better."

His words left like a whisper, but they echoed in my head. My mind started to wonder if that was even what he said or if I'd just imagined it. It almost didn't matter. His fingers pressed against my cheek. I wondered if I'd missed my cue. Before I could properly decide how I wanted to lean in, he made the choice for me. The arm that was still around my shoulder exerted a gentle pulling force that brought me to him. Our lips met.

I jumped and parted from him as my phone vibrated in my back pocket.

"I'm sorry!"

He laughed and brushed the hair from his face.

Any luck?

The text from Jordyn came through. I sent a thumbs up in response.

"Let's get out of here and to somewhere more private. I only have a bit though, got some papers to catch up on."

"I could help with that. I have a little bit of work of my own."

He smiled and grabbed my backpack before I was able to get my coat on.

"I can carry that, you know."

"I know."

That was all he said as he walked to the door and opened it, motioning for me to go through. I bit my lip and thanked him with a nod. My walk might have looked more like a giddy skip to anyone who may have been watching, but I didn't care. Why should I be ashamed of my happiness?

Chapter Twenty-Two

The week soared by. No exams this time, but the assignments seemed to really stack up as the end of the semester drew near. I met with Jordyn every afternoon when classes ended to polish up her poem. When practice ended, I would head out and meet up with Chase. We ended our bad habit of eating out every time we were together, heading to the computer lab instead and grabbing a pod so we could talk, do class work, and find chances to kiss without it being too much of a public display of affection. Winter approached and my dorm room was not an option, so we made do.

The day before her reading, Jordyn was hyperventilating yet again.

"You'll be fine. You've already done it once before."

"Yeah, but you weren't there to hear the crickets after I finished."

"It could not have been that bad."

"Crickets!"

I rolled my eyes and rested my head on my hands, elbows digging into my knees as the weight pressed down. I glanced at the copy she'd made of her poem as my own personal editor copy. I squiggled in some notes here and there of sentences that sounded awkward or disjointed as I read it in my head, but when she read it out loud, I crossed out every note I had.

"I seriously doubt that no one clapped or snapped or whatever it is you do," I said, eyes meeting hers which were so wide they looked like they were about to fall from her sockets.

Jordyn pressed her palms against the sides of her head and chattered her teeth together. She paced back and forth, throwing a piece of cheddar popcorn in her mouth every time she arrived back at her desk.

"Anyways, you know you'll have at least one pair of hands clapping you on!"

"Yes, if you decide to actually show up this time. Jokes aside, you would clap even if I repeated the same word over and over again."

"Hey, if the changes in inflection are on point, why not? Really though, I've read this piece hundreds of times and have heard you recite it multiple times on top of that. You really think I'd let you get up in front of a bunch of people with a stupid poem? You gotta give me more credit than that."

Jordyn sighed loud enough to shake the walls and fell back into her bed.

My phone vibrated on the floor next to me, his face popping up on the screen. I scrunched my nose and quickly sent him a message.

I'll call back later, a bit busy. You're okay, right? No emergency?

I waited a moment as my heart started to race wondering what sort of accident or incident he possibly found himself in.

Practice ended early. Home game tomorrow. Just wanted to hear your voice.

His message was followed by a smiley face emoji. I returned his figurative smile.

"You are too cute," Jordyn mumbled with her pillow near her face as she peeked at me from over the side of the bed.

"Thanks?"

I put my phone down and started to read through her poem again.

"No, but seriously. I'm happy for you. You deserve to find someone who treats you right."

"Don't we all?"

Jordyn smiled and bounced up, excitement that she forgot she had eating at her. She grabbed her phone and flashed me a guy's profile pic.

"Who is that?" I asked with a high pitch to my tone. My eyebrows raised in interest.

"He plays bass for We Hunt the Monsters. Sent me a friend request."

"Have you accepted it?"

"No..." she said while creating a hollow sound in her mouth. "I'm too nervous."

"Girl, now is your chance. Go for it!"

"I don't want to be *that* girl."

"Be that girl!"

I jumped up and leapt into her bed, wrapping my arms about her. Shaking her to her senses, I reached for her phone that she had set beside her and shoved it in her face.

"Accept now or I'll do it for you!"

Jordyn grimaced, her eyes betraying her excitement, and clicked through the steps to open up her app and accept the friend request. As her finger clicked the button, she threw her phone to the ground, shoved her face into the pillow, and squealed.

I laughed and jumped from the bed, picking up her phone to look through his profile. Matt was a nice guy, a tad bit more timid than the others, but he really had an ear for music. I remembered humming how the notes of Jordyn's song would play out, and he was able to get down the melody and develop a harmony from there. Most of his pictures were of him with his bass guitar, at concerts and events. In honesty, I could have never found a more perfect guy for Jordyn myself.

"Now message him!"

I threw her phone back up to her. She flinched as if it were a bee flying in her direction.

"Absolutely the fuck not!"

"Can't be scarier than reading a poem in front of a crowd of people."

"It was literally like fifteen people there and most of them were just there for a friend. Probably only two people actually listened."

"And Matt's just one guy, so see? Easier."

Jordyn stuck out her tongue and mockingly laughed.

We went back and forth for a bit, her finally sending a simple hello. When leaving, I sprinted down the steps, phone in hand, trying to dial his number as I went. The dial tone started up.

"Hello?"

"Hey, where are you? Just finished what I was doing."

"You been working out? You sound out of breath."

"I literally just climbed down some stairs. I'm out of shape, I get it."

He laughed and clicked his tongue.

"I'm walking with Dean to buy some stuff. You need anything? We'll meet up in a bit."

"I just need you to hurry because what I really need is some us time."

He let out a breathy chuckle.

"Me, too. Let me call you back here in like ten minutes. I'll come get you, if you just want to wait on the couches."

"Sounds like a plan."

"Kay. See ya."

"Yep."

My heart always fluttered before, during, and after speaking with him. Just having him in my mind was enough to make me all joyous and happy, as if nothing else in the world mattered.

I laid on the sofa with clear sights to the door he always approached and waited. Like Sleeping Beauty for her prince, I waited for him to sweep me off my feet and take me to some fairytale land where his touch was enough to wake me and his kisses magical enough to revitalize.

When he arrived, we headed to his room for a movie and some privacy. As much as we hadn't planned on it, we both fell asleep while lying on his bed. I think I was out before the movie's name even crossed the screen. I hadn't realized until it was past midnight and credits had already finished, the title screen staring back at me. I grabbed the remote which had lodged itself into my stomach, turned off the screen, and threw it to the floor. My movements and the thud caused him to wake.

"Shit," he groggily whispered, hands rubbing across his eyes. "I swore I wouldn't do this."

"Same."

I pulled the blanket up further about my arms as a chill air made my hairs stand on end.

"Let's get you back so you can sleep."

"Are you insane? It's freezing outside, and you've got a game tomorrow. I'll just sleep on the floor."

"No, you're insane if you think I'd let you sleep on the floor. I'll do it."

"Okay, hear me out. We're mature adults here." I licked my lips as my heart skipped a beat. The butterflies in my stomach started to swarm. "We're both already comfortable here so why don't we just go back to sleep? Like stay as we are?"

Chase's hand fell on my hip, causing me to bend my neck to see him from over my shoulder as we both laid on our sides.

"If you're okay with that, that's fine. I didn't want you to be uncomfortable."

"I'm actually very comfortable," I whispered and nestled up against his pillow with the blankets brought near to my face.

His arm wrapped about my waist, the only thing between me and the blanket, yet his arm kept me warm. It radiated its own heat. With a gentle tug back, I felt my body cradle into his own. Pressed softly into one another, I didn't know if I'd ever want to sleep alone again.

The next morning, we woke at the same time, eating a small breakfast and making plans to meet up again in the afternoon after the game. I had to meet up with Jordyn outside the gates, so I wouldn't be alone in the stands cheering him on. She brought blankets and hid candy inside of her coat pockets, not wanting to pay those concession prices. I laughed but didn't refuse offering up one of my own pockets for some brownie bites.

Despite the chill air of early afternoon, we cheered him and the team on, neither of us understanding what we were looking at. At least with the stream I watched previously, the commentators let me know when a play was good or bad. At this point, all I knew were the uniform colors I didn't want to have possession of the ball. I clenched my fists tight as he swooped the ball away from their opponent. Running it down the field and passing to an open teammate, he assisted in the first and only goal of the game. Whether I made Jordyn deaf or the other way around, side eyes met us from the few others who were in the stands, as if our excitement was a bit too overboard. When the team pulled away from their celebration to set up for the next kick, Chase turned to us and pointed at me. I swooned.

After the game, Jordyn and I ran to the concession stands for hot chocolate before they closed, our fingers numb from the cold and feeling as though they'd break and fall off. Every sip burned as it touched the tongue and trickled down my throat. It was so satisfying, warming me from the inside out.

As evening set in, the day darker at this hour as winter drew to its peak, we all met up at The Lounge. Chase wrapped an arm about my shoulders as we took our seats at a table. Jordyn and Matt sat across from us. Jordyn grabbed tight to her stomach, nerves and nausea eating away at her as the time drew near. Matt and I tried to talk her down from the cliff.

"Just shake out the nerves," Matt suggested, offering her a sip of his lemon water. "Before every show, I've got this ritual that helps calm me down and focus before going onstage. I count through five things that I look forward to. It can be anything. Actual plans or things you just want to do in the future. I start every sentence with 'I look forward to' and just list them off one by one."

"I look forward to this being over." Jordyn squeezed her hands together in a prayer position with closed eyes. When she opened them, she looked about and sighed. "That didn't help."

"It's not like you're making a wish to a genie," I said. "Just distract yourself."

"And miss my name being called? That might embarrass me more than someone laughing during my reading."

"And if someone laughs, so what? Art is created by the artist and meant to be interpreted by the audience. If someone finds it funny then hey, at least you've touched someone with your words."

"I guess."

"Next up is Jordyn Wilson!" The MC announced.

Everyone at our table clapped but her. She stood and sulked to the stage. When she arrived at the mic, we still hadn't stopped clapping and cheering. She licked her lips and gulped down her nerves.

She hit every word and every emphasis. Memorized to the beat, to the emotion, I found tears drawn to my eyes in the power she possessed, in how proud I was of her. Chase's hand squeezed my shoulder and pulled me in. I rested my hand on his thigh and felt as though I was drowning in happiness.

My eyes wandered The Lounge, taking it all in. I wanted to remember this scene for decades to come. No matter what happened, this was the moment when it seemed that anything and everything was possible.

As the last word of her poem left her, Jordyn nodded to the mic as thanks and tried to race away before the inevitable but was too late. I jumped to my feet, followed by Chase and Matt. We applauded and screamed, Chase whistling in a way that could probably be heard in the next state over. Jordyn beamed at the reception, eyeing the others in the club who were also offering her a standing ovation.

She sprinted to the table in her embarrassment, and I jumped at her, wrapping my arms about her.

"You are such an inspiration," I whispered in her ear.

A tear streamed down her cheek.

This was it. I'd found it. My eyes met Chase from over Jordyn's shoulder. His smile spelled so much more than just a friend. So much more than being just a best friend.

This was the balance.

This was happiness.

Chapter Twenty-Three

"What'd you get?" his arms wrapped about my torso as I sat in my chair, leaning into my laptop.

I bit my bottom lip, waiting for the screen to load, the swirling wheel of death staring at me. Mocking me. Words and numbers filled the page, and I scrolled as fast as I could to the bottom.

Another A.

"I passed!"

His lips pressed into my cheek, my lips jealous of their placement. I set my computer down, turned to him, and stole another before he could get away. Relief filled me, knowing that my first semester went so well. The stress of not only diving into what would be the start of a new life but also the drama along the way dissolved, and I nestled myself into his arms for a warm embrace.

We moved to my bed and kissed, time and time again. His lips played around mine, moving to my cheeks, my neck, playing with my ear. I giggled and clutched to his shirt, pulling him closer to me and leaning into every playful kiss he had to offer.

I didn't have to worry about being caught, about her seeing us and commenting on every little thing we said or did. Sara had left right after finishing her last exam, her bags packed the night before so she could catch the earliest plane possible. An escape from this hellhole, she claimed. And that also meant that her side of the room was a mess. She decided she'd save the cleaning for when she got back from winter break. Granted, she probably knew after a couple of days I'd grow sick of it and just clean it myself. She'd be right.

We caught our breath as we pulled apart, his smile the most precious source of joy in my life. I took his hand in mine and squeezed as tight as I could.

"Hey," he laughed, though he did not try to take it from me. "You're a lot stronger than you think you are."

"I just wanted to know that this is real."

"You've said that a million and one times already. This is as real as it gets."

"I know." I released a breathy giggle followed by a profound exhale. "I just keep fearing that one of these times it won't be. I don't know what I'd do."

"Well, you don't have to think about that for now. I've got you. You've got me. We have each other."

I rolled on top of him and wrapped my arms about his neck, compressing our bodies together. He raised his arms as if to embrace but rather started tickling my sides. I laughed uncontrollably and rolled to the floor, him following me there in an attempt to soften my fall. We both laughed.

A knock at the door startled us both. I jumped up and, after fixing my hair, opened it. A giftbag covered her face, but I knew it was her before she had the chance to drop it.

"I bring gifts!" Jordyn sang as she entered and dropped two giftbags to the floor.

I ran to my closet and took out her present, passing it to her. Chase waved to her with a smile, and she returned it.

"You two are seriously going to spend your break here?" Jordyn asked, taking a seat on the floor and peering up at me.

"I have no interest in seeing either side of my family," I said, sitting beside her and offering her an open box of cookies Chase brought me that morning. She took one and bit down with a satisfied moan. "Better here than there. This was my escape from them in the first place."

"And you, too, Chase? Family issues?"

Chase laughed and tossed back his hair as he sat on the edge of the bed.

"Nah, just trying to save up my money. Didn't want to splurge on a round trip ticket. Besides, I've got everything I need right here."

Our eyes met with delighted joy. Jordyn faked a gag and laughed.

"Whatever rocks your boat, I guess."

"You and Matt gonna meet up over the holidays?" I asked, taking a cookie for myself and savoring the heavenly combination of chocolate and peanut butter chips.

"We have plans for New Year's. There's apparently some huge celebration in his hometown. He was gonna perform at a local club too that night. We'll see what happens."

"Well, I hope you all have a blast."

"You know we will."

Jordyn stood with her gift in hand and offered me a hug.

"I have to get going. Parents are coming to pick me up and I haven't packed anything yet."

I embraced her in a tight squeeze.

"Text me when you're heading out then and when you get home. Just want to know you made it safely."

"Copy that, mom."

We laughed. She offered a hug to Chase, who hesitantly accepted, then flashed a peace sign as she closed the door.

I jumped on the bed beside Chase the moment the door clicked and pulled him down. His hand fell on my waist and the temptation hit us again. Kissing wasn't the only way we communicated, but it was definitely our strongest love language.

My phone rang, causing us both to flinch. I leapt from the bed and scouted the desk from the sound, the many scattered papers and gift wrappings from the gifts I'd received covering the space. When at long last I found it, the screen showed my sister's name and picture.

"Who is it?"

"My sister. That's weird." I clicked to accept the call, which was over video, and adjusted myself until I was in good light.

"Hey, there. How are you? Things end up working out through the end of the year?"

My sister leaned back in a chair, exposing the small bump that was her stomach, rubbing it with her hand.

"Yeah. Everything actually worked out perfectly, or as close to it as I could have hoped. Aced all my classes. Made some memories. Everyone tried to scare us with these horror stories of freshman year, but the first semester really wasn't so bad."

"I'm glad it worked out. Like I've said before, better for you than for me."

"You still have morning sickness?"

My sister laughed and peered down at her stomach for a moment.

"That and about ten other new symptoms. Truly I will never understand how any woman or childbearing person would want to do this more than once. But you'll learn, too, sooner or later."

Chase choked on the water he had been drinking and wiped away at his mouth. I laughed and glanced at him, our eyes meeting with amusement. My sister furrowed her brow.

"Sorry," I laughed, trying to fill her in. "My boyfriend heard that and thought it was funny."

"Ohhh. His name is Chase, right? Hi, Chase! How are you?"

"I'm good," he called out. "And you?"

"Oh, just fabulous, thanks for asking. So, are you going to see mom for the holidays?"

"No, I'm staying here. Don't want any more drama for a while."

"Understood. Might scar Chase too if he met her. Give it a bit more time."

We shared a moment of silence, gazing at one another as if trying to decipher any tragedies or issues the other wasn't revealing. It was a sisterly thing, analyzing every strand of hair, every wrinkle, what she was wearing, any little thing that would signal depression or sickness. At long last, we both released a simultaneous profound exhale.

"Well, just wanted to make sure you survived your first semester."

"I might not have if it wasn't for you."

"You gotta give yourself more credit. You pushed to be better. I could have said any number of words, but you had to decide to make that jump."

"I needed someone to pull me off the ground though first. Rising from the fall is so much easier when there is someone who cares. Anyways, love you. Stay safe."

"Love you, too."

We hung up. I looked up from my phone to see Chase smiling at me. He had laid his empty water bottle on the bed, and it pointed in my direction. A cheesy grin formed on my face as my heart accelerated and warmed to the love I was drowning in.

ABOUT THE AUTHOR

Elle Oaks is a pen name for her contemporary fiction works. She also writes under the name M. A. Morales in the speculative fiction genre.

Check out our website to see our other works. If you are a writer or author, check out our blog for tips and tricks for your writing and self-publishing journey.

Please leave a rating and review, especially if you enjoyed it :P

www.ingramcontent.com/pod-product-compliance
Lightning Source LLC
Chambersburg PA
CBHW050849180626
46814CB00007B/2688